Crawling into his bed, surrounded by the smell of him, Sibyl couldn't possibly sleep.

She listened to the shower across the hall. She imagined Trace in there, washing off all that blood and sweat. Why hadn't it bothered her more?

Because it's his.

The horror she'd felt when she'd thought him hurt or dead...the odd ache in her chest when he'd all but dared her to be disgusted by him.... She didn't need experience she didn't have, or the IQ she did, to face what this had become. She needed only a little courage.

She was falling in love with Trace Beaudry. Trace LaSalle-Beaudry...no. That confused things too much. Let him be just Trace.

★★★

Dear Reader,

If this is your first Evelyn Vaughn title, thank you for checking me out! If, however, you've been looking for *Underground Warrior* since *Knight in Blue Jeans* came out, then I also thank you for your patience. I've been writing more slowly lately, which, unfortunately, resulted in a long wait for you. My apologies.

Trace and Sibyl's story gave me the chance to explore human resilience, from that of a girl falsely imprisoned to that of a city striving to rebuild itself after disaster. If New Orleans can keep going, then why can't the rest of us?

I hope all of you enjoy *Underground Warrior!*

Evelyn Vaughn

EVELYN VAUGHN

Underground Warrior

ROMANTIC
SUSPENSE

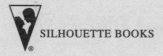 SILHOUETTE BOOKS

Recycling programs for this product may not exist in your area.

ISBN-13: 978-0-373-27712-4

UNDERGROUND WARRIOR

Copyright © 2011 by Yvonne Jocks

This edition published by arrangement with Harlequin Books S.A.

For questions and comments about the quality of this book please contact us at Customer_eCare@Harlequin.ca.

® and TM are trademarks of Harlequin Books S.A., used under license. Trademarks indicated with ® are registered in the United States Patent and Trademark Office, the Canadian Trade Marks Office and in other countries.

Visit Silhouette Books at www.eHarlequin.com

Printed in U.S.A.

EVELYN VAUGHN

believes in many magicks, particularly the magic of storytelling. She has written fiction since she could print words, first publishing in a newspaper contest at the age of twelve. Thirty(ish) years later, she's publishing her eighteenth novel. Evelyn loves movies and videos, and is an unapologetic TV addict. Luckily, her imaginary friends and her cats seem to get along.

Evelyn loves to talk about stories and characters, especially her own. Please write her at Yvaughn@aol.com.

I owe many thanks for *Underground Warrior,* including
Juliet Burns, Paige Wheeler, Natashya Wilson,
Patience Smith, Shana Smith, Kayli Rhodes,
the Texas Read'ems (who helped me come up with
the idea for the Blade Keepers) and the First Thursday
Romance Reader Bookclub (who kept me going).
Because of them, I dedicate this book to my readers.
You complete me!

Prologue

"He said to come alone," said the pretty woman.

Her partner answered, "They *always* say to come alone."

Silently spying on the couple from her corner of the sun-drenched restaurant patio, Sibyl analyzed her discomfort. It wasn't fear. Fear she understood—had understood since, as a twelve-year-old, she'd watched her world end. *Red-and-blue flashing lights. A pounding on the door. Mama's cry...*

Sibyl pushed the memories safely behind a wall of reason. She'd come here for information. Exposure was the one thing her enemies—a secret society of powerful men, of killers—feared.

A pounding gavel. "The court finds Isabel Daine

guilty of arson and manslaughter." A public defender too drunk to sugarcoat it. "*Some people in this town, you just can't fight.*"

Some people. Why not just say secret society? *The Comitatus.* And no people willing to admit who really started the fire that killed her father.

The wealthy, powerful society wouldn't allow it. Perhaps Sibyl could catalog her newest discomfort as frustration. Arden Leigh, socialite daughter of a Dallas Comitatus leader, had broken her emailed promise. Sibyl—anonymous under the handle of Vox07—*had* specified that they meet alone. Instead, Arden brought a suitor. Despite his old T-shirt and faded jeans, his posture and speech patterns bespoke wealth. Power. *Comitatus.*

"Thank heavens I have a big, strong man to protect me," Arden teased her beau. Sibyl's stomach twisted as she watched. She had to get out of there.

Across a wide parking lot, a yellow-and-white light-rail train slid to a halt with a ringing of bells. While disembarking passengers distracted the pretty couple, Sibyl scribbled a simple, angry note onto a strip of paper placemat—*Liars!*

Risky or not, she couldn't just ignore people lying, cheating and getting their own way at the expense of others. Not powerful secret societies descended from bloody conquerors like Charlemagne or Genghis Khan. Not beauty queens with false smiles and doting, disguised lovers. Not anyone.

Swallowing back her hurt, Sibyl stood to leave the

patio. She dropped the note surreptitiously into the socialite's purse as she passed.

Suddenly, the woman's partner blocked the one exit. "Hiya, Vox."

Sibyl spun and ran, vaulting the iron fencing of the patio and racing across a hot, Texas parking lot toward the train stop. She dodged surprised tourists. She threaded between cars. The 2:18 pulled away from the historic district, but she could lose herself in the crowd heading for El Centro Community College just beyond, if she…could…just….

The obstacle of a second man, angling toward her from behind the train stop's handicap access ramp, forced her to a stumbling stop. *No….*

Tailored suit, despite the August heat wave. Expensive sunglasses. An air of absolute entitlement, even for nobility. More Comitatus.

If her years of uncovering every scrap of information she could find on them had taught her nothing else, it taught her how to recognize their agents.

Fight. No, move. No—fight! Sibyl pivoted—but here came the couple who'd chased her. She fell an instinctive step back and spotted a third enemy—privileged walk despite his cheap clothing and beach-blond hair—closing in from another direction. They'd surrounded her. They'd won. Again.

"It's all right, honey!" lied the beauty queen, reaching for her. "You can trust—"

The scream of a train whistle drowned her out.

Sybil spun to face the light-rail train that loomed

down on her with an urgent wail of warning. A blow hurled her into brick pavement.

Then…? *Silence.*

Wouldn't a train's impact hurt more? She curled her hand on the hot bricks beneath her…and smelled the earthy, unmistakable scent of man on top of her, sheltering her. She felt the rub of coarse skin on her bare arms, of denim on her bare legs. Despite the gruff cursing over the screech of metal brakes, she felt safe.

Literally. *Someone saved her.*

Someone who weighed almost as much as a train, even so.

Opening her eyes, Sibyl turned her head to the man who rolled off her. His size momentarily blocked the sun and blue sky. Swarthy, she noted. Angry…she'd been angering men for a long time now. This one, at least, had some cause.

He could have died. Which meant he, at least, didn't want her silenced.

"What the hell were you doing?" her savior demanded, cutting through her shock. His accent held the familiar trace of Louisiana—rural Louisiana. He pulled her effortlessly upward with one huge, rough hand around hers, and she let him. "When a train's about to hit you, you move, you don't just stand there!"

Sibyl barely reached his broad chest, even in her cowboy boots. The muscles of his shoulders bulged under his T-shirt; the muscles of his thick arms she could see for herself under sun-browned skin. Substantial, she thought. Blue collar, not white collar. A two-day beard shadowed his jaw. Primitive. And he'd risked his life for her.

A strange sensation filled her. After a decade alone, she searched for a label, then surprised herself. *Trust?* She trusted him. Completely.

"Oh, thank God!" Arden Leigh put on a surprisingly good show of concern. So did her beau and the blond man, with their prep school postures and thrift store clothes. The one man who'd dressed Comitatus-wealthy had vanished. *Safe.* "We didn't mean to frighten you."

"I guess you just don't have the way with women that Trace does." The blond man laughed. Sibyl's hero grunted casual disgust, but she didn't hear his reply.

They were together. This man—Trace—who seemed like the anti-Comitatus, knew people she'd assumed were her enemies. And yet, as the others crowded around her, Sibyl instinctively pressed back against her savior's solid body. Fear, she understood. It shouldn't stop her from finding out more about these not-quite-Comitatus types…or their friend. *If* she could trust him.

Needing time, needing proof, Sibyl rolled her eyes upward and dropped into a feigned faint, like some damsel in distress.

Her hero caught her, swept her into his hard arms, held her close to his broad, warm chest—and growled an unheroic, "Crap."

Sibyl had no intention of analyzing the feelings that swept past her wall of reason, this time.

Some truths were just too dangerous to consider.

Chapter 1

"Doubt separates people...it is a sword that kills."
—Buddha

New Orleans, three months later

Trace Beaudry didn't consider himself a big thinker.

Big? Hell, yeah.

A thinker? Not so much.

But even he couldn't ignore the significance of finally entering his ancestors' once grand, now ruined, home. This house could have been his inheritance if he'd been smarter, classier, *better.* He'd tried. He'd failed. Now the house sat empty and rotting.

And here Trace stood, the bastard end of his genetic line—hefting the sledgehammer that would take it down.

Even through the bandanna across his face, even

with a fresh stick of peppermint gum in his mouth, the fancy "bungalow" stank as thick and awful as any other New Orleans flood house. It had stood empty for years before Hurricane Katrina turned even nice areas of New Orleans into Southern Lake Pontchartrain. But what really trashed the building were the months it sat untouched, afterward. The Judge—Trace couldn't think of the man he'd first met on his fifteenth birthday as a *father*—had apparently fought the city's attempts to force his hand. For once, the Judge lost.

And now his illegitimate son crossed the threshold at last.

Dirt and flyspecks darkened lead cathedral windows. Deadly black mold laced across layers of brittle wallpaper that sagged like bunting from an equally grimy ceiling. Inches of bug-infested filth carpeted both the floor and the museum-quality furniture strewn about by forgotten floodwaters. A ceiling fan's blades wilted like an upside-down flower, pulled downward as those waters had receded, and then dried like that, as much as anything ever dried in Louisiana. A rat scurried up the curved, wrought-iron staircase.

Trace knuckled his hard hat back as he took it all in—and snorted.

"Eh?" asked Alain, who'd grown up in the same trailer park as Trace. He ran the construction crew hired for this gut job. He'd bid extra low, just to see this little piece of Trace's fancy-schmancy history.

Trace shook his head, at a loss for the right words. Irony? Symbolism? Karma? He didn't want to call on the botched education that his embarrassing attempt at legitimacy, at life as a LaSalle, had bought him. He'd tried living in his father's world. He'd failed. End of story. Now he settled for, "Life's funny, huh?"

Then the six-man team set about knocking down every bit of the house except the frame and foundation. They started by emptying it, piling up mounds of trash and recyclables at the distant, weed-shrouded curb. Then they shoveled muck off the floor into wheelbarrows to cart outside. Only later could they break down the walls, pull out the insulation and leave only the bungalow's frame to be rebuilt. Trace liked the honest, hard work of it—no polish or sophistication required. No stupid rituals or secrecy, either. He liked sweating and lifting and pushing his fighter's body to the limit without hurting anyone. He liked not thinking.

This was why he'd left his friends—fellow outcasts from their fathers' world of privilege and power—back in Dallas, once they started making noises about fixing that world. They thought too much.

Trace was a man of action.

"So much for curb appeal, eh?" Alain joked from the street, hours later. The once-white wall had grayed to the waterline, with a spray-painted cross tagging the date of its inspection. Its ancient oak and magnolia trees stood dead, killed by poisons in the long-standing water as much as by drowning. But at least outside, in the humid Louisiana November, they could all breathe and switch to fresh gum.

"Yeah," snorted Trace, strangely dissatisfied whenever he stopped for too long. "We should hire out as decorators, huh?"

Which is when Bubba called them to "come see." So they pulled their bandannas back up like Old West bank robbers and headed back in.

Bubba had torn big swaths of moldy wallpaper off the foyer wall.

"Smart," mocked Trace, of the extra dust. "The air wasn't nasty enough."

Then he saw the picture—the *fresco,* he labeled it in a brief echo from his attempt at higher education—that Bubba had uncovered.

That weight he'd first felt in his chest this morning, that searching for words? It tripled. The plaster painting was ruined, darkened with mold here, torn away with the paper there. But enough remained for them to make out the basics. It showed a field of battle, with banners and horses and knights in armor, some upright, some dead. They all wore swords. One, standing, wore a crown—the king. Another, dead or dying beside the king, had some kind of drinking horn lying near him. Maybe the king had poisoned him. Trace wouldn't put that past his father's ancestors.

God forbid rich folks paint the foot soldiers on their wall, right? Or the peasants who shined their armor and cleaned up after their horses. Or, for that matter, their women.

"Whattaya think?" asked Bubba. "Maybe you're related to one of those old guys, huh, LaSalle?"

"I'm not a LaSalle," Trace growled—and picked up the nearest sledgehammer. "My ma's a Beaudry."

"Whoa!" shouted Alain. "Safety goggles!"

Trace swung. The heavy, iron head of the hammer bit

hard into the painted plaster. Its impact ran up his arms. Pieces of kings and knights fell off the wall, leaving fresh, pale scars on the mold-stained scene. Still, too much remained, so Trace swung again.

Then again. Damn, it felt good. He liked denying the heritage that had felt like a fairy tale, like a lie come too late and never as promised.

He liked unleashing his strength, no-holds-barred. He might be a bull, but this was no china shop. This was man-versus-wall.

And the wall freaking went down.

Goodbye, king. Goodbye, dead knight. Goodbye, trees and horses and hills and sky. Goodbye, secret society of overlords and servility that should've died out centuries ago.

Au revoir, LaSalle fairy tale.

Within moments, Trace had reduced the whole water-stained ruin of a wall to rubble. He was breathing hard. His whole body vibrated from the exercise. This felt better than the endorphin rush after a long run, a hard workout, an underground fight.

And then, half-hidden behind clumps of former wall in the settling plaster dust, he saw it. And everything kind of went still.

A…sword?

He crouched down to one knee, his ears ringing in the sudden silence, and reached out—but hesitated to touch the thing. Instead, almost respectfully, he moved clumps of wall off it.

Yeah. That was a sword, all right. Not flared like a pirate's, like the one his fellow outcast Smith Donnell had gotten hold of a few months back. And not slim and light, like the ones they'd used when he took fencing as a PE credit, back at that damned college he'd hated.

This was a *real* sword. A warrior's sword.

It stretched longer and wider than a yardstick, straight as a line. Its hilt formed a cross. Despite never paying attention in history, Trace had a sudden flash of a knight stabbing the sword's blade into the earth, then kneeling to pray to the temporary cross he'd created.

Kind of like how he was kneeling, right now. Weird coincidence.

"Whoa!" exclaimed Alain, reaching for it. "What the hell?"

"Mine!" snarled Trace. "Go!" And his friends immediately backed off. Probably because Trace sounded insane. This had to be a LaSalle antique. He didn't want anything to do with the LaSalles. He was a Beaudry.

But sometimes a guy just knew, whether it made sense or not, that something belonged to him. And that sword, lying sealed behind the wall for God knew how long? *That sword was his.*

His.

Which somehow made him think of the exact person who could answer some questions about it for him.

Click. Down the once tree-lined street, a private investigator sat in his car snapping picture after picture. Grunts in hard hats hauling scrap iron and rotting furniture to the curb? *Click.* Guys stopping to catch their breath under dead trees before going back into the bungalow? *Click.*

He smoked. He drank coffee. He peed into a jar. And he photographed. Thank God digital photos were so cheap. He could just save it all onto a DVD, instead of the old days that required prints. He didn't know what the blue blood who'd hired him cared about this stinking, ugly cleanup; it was still happening all over New Orleans. But if Charles was willing to pay, he was willing to document.

Still, he doubted they'd see anything interesting. *Click.*

Sibyl reached the top of the apartment's spiral staircase—a trendy loft bedroom, complete with old brick walls and exposed ductwork—and realized she didn't know why she'd gone there. She turned in a circle, using the loft's vantage to worriedly eye the rest of the apartment. Of course it looked perfect, from its concrete floors to its wall-of-glass windows overlooking the Trinity River levee. But nobody would ever believe it was hers.

What had she done? Hadn't she gone to great lengths to avoid visitors?

A child genius, Sibyl—then Isabel Daine—had gotten a scholarship to the prestigious New Orleans Preparatory Academy by the age of ten. She must have known what secret societies were, even then—could probably have recited the *Oxford English Dictionary*'s etymology of the phrase. But she would have more easily believed in Santa Claus, which, based on the scientific and temporal improbabilities, she had not.

She'd been too busy studying, too busy "looking

ahead," as her father had always advised. He'd taken a job as a night watchman at the school. Academy students lived far above her family's middle-class income. By the age of twelve, Sibyl was set to graduate first in her class. She had full rides to Yale, Harvard, even Oxford, hers for the choosing.

Then came the pounding at the front door—she woke to a strobe of red-and-blue lights entering her dark bedroom. A fire at the academy had killed her father.

A fire the police said she'd set.

Evidence came from nowhere—classmates and even professors suddenly labeled her as sullen, resentful, unpredictable. Her? The school paper produced a "rejected editorial" she'd never actually written.

Even her mother had begun to doubt her. "Darling, if you were so unhappy there," she'd said through the Plexiglas that separated visitors from prisoners.

"I *wasn't*," Isabel had screamed, so the guards ended the visit.

She'd been too young for a jury trial, so the verdict rested on a certain Judge LaSalle. He convicted her of arson and manslaughter. Sibyl lost her graduation with honors. She lost Yale and Harvard and Oxford. She lost her daddy, who'd been so excited for her, and her mother, who couldn't bear up under legal bills, scandal and doubts. She gave up her very name, her identity.

Sibyl lost everything except her genius. From the girls' penitentiary, getting computer access to earn her GED and several undergraduate degrees, Sibyl had thrown every bit of her IQ into hacking the truth. She couldn't tell for sure who had set the fire. But eventually, she learned who had covered it up.

Conspiracy theorists warned of the Masons. The Trilateral Commission. The Bildebergers. But far better hidden lay a secret society called the Comitatus.

Sibyl learned as much as she could from behind bars and then, after her release at the age of eighteen, she uncovered the rest. Peripheral comments in ancient manuscripts. Lost journals she'd uncovered. The testimony of other, frightened victims. Personal correspondence that people like Judge LaSalle thought inaccessible. Nothing was safe from her quest.

Now twenty-two years old, Sibyl considered herself as much an expert on the powerful, world-wide Comitatus as existed outside their control. Name a powerful family, and they'd likely belonged. Capet and Valois. Aragon and Castille. Plantagenet and Stuart. Just in case she'd foolishly thought heroes still existed, after what she'd been through.

But she needed to know more. Comitatus members were wealthy, blue-blooded and influential. But Sibyl meant to take them down—if she could survive that long. So she took precautions.

Sibyl never, ever answered her disposable, untraceable, prepaid cell phone—if she wanted to talk after hearing the message, she would call back. *Just because you're paranoid doesn't mean they aren't after you.* Especially one small, lonesome woman versus a worldwide secret society. The people who had her latest number, she could count on two hands—as if someone with her IQ needed to finger count.

The people she would call back, she could (figuratively) count on one hand.

Trace Beaudry was the first person she'd not only called back, but invited to visit. Her inability to decide why worried her. She knew why she trusted him; that went back to the risking-his-life-to-save-hers business. It factored in data she'd gathered in the few days she'd spent helping him and his friends, after that rescue. His friends had *former* Comitatus backgrounds. Their claimed rejection of the society explained both their poverty and their foolish goal to somehow salvage said society. But Trace had no such background at all. Trace was a Beaudry. Despite being a frighteningly good hacker, Sibyl could find no reference to a Comitatus member or family line under that name.

And she'd looked. *See: paranoid.*

But even meeting non-Comitatus men here, alone, fell under the heading of "Things movies teach you not to do." Unless the movie was a romance. This wasn't a romance. Sibyl wouldn't know what to do with a—

Drinks! She spiraled back down the stairs to the large, open kitchen to look into the formerly empty, stainless steel refrigerator. Again.

It held a six-pack of every major soda she could find and nothing else. Sibyl suspected Trace wouldn't want any of it—he was just coming to ask a few questions about her research. Besides, he'd seemed like a beer drinker. She'd considered getting beer for him, but knew she'd get carded because of her height. Although even her real ID showed her as legal, Sibyl didn't like using it. She didn't like people looking too closely at her.

Trace would look at her, if not closely. Now she ran to the mirror beside the front door and stopped bouncing on the balls of her feet long enough to narrow her eyes at her reflection. Thank heavens she'd let Arden Leigh take her on that girls-day-out to the Galleria last month, which had somehow became a makeover. Sibyl had seen it as a way to coax information out of the beauty queen, who'd only recently learned about the secret society but might eventually allow Sibyl to go through her father's papers. Also, Arden's father had recently passed, and the socialite seemed to take comfort in playing fairy godmother.

Sibyl knew from losing fathers—not that she admitted that to Arden. But letting someone drape her in a pink silk cape and massage her scalp while shampooing and then trimming her long hair had seemed a minor sacrifice.

Today she used very little of the makeup Arden had given her, but her hair did seem shinier, smoother. That was something. The oversize shirt in a boxy plaid of autumn colors looked casual but stylish—which, to judge by the price Arden paid, it was. The brown leggings felt comfortable enough. Sibyl had had to buy nail polish remover just to clean her fingers after their mani-pedi, but she'd left her toes alone, and the pretty copper color hadn't chipped.

She blinked at her reflection, then looked down. *Toes.* That's why she'd gone upstairs. Boots!

But Trace rapped on the door—it had to be him—and she was out of time.

"Breathe," Sibyl whispered to herself. She'd faced

down gang members, in juvie, if reluctantly. "Oxygen is fuel." Surely she could face one guy. One good guy, a hero even. *Her* hero.

With a groan that had nothing to do with physical effort, she pushed aside the loft's sliding door—and there he stood. Trace hadn't changed in the months since he'd fled Dallas, maybe fled her. At six-four, he still towered over her. His hair, a much darker brown than hers, looked like he'd never been subjected to pink capes or scalp massages. Considering her belief that wealth corrupted people, that was a plus. So were his swarthy laborer's tan and his worn jeans and T-shirt, stretched to accommodate his breadth. He didn't seem to have shaved for days; give him another week, and he'd have a full beard.

Yes—this was her Trace. His constancy somehow soothed her.

Only belatedly did she notice that he was carrying in one hand something the size of a handful of canes, wrapped in a stained tarp.

He seemed oddly distracted as he said, "Hey, Short-stuff. Can I come in?"

Belatedly, Sibyl backed out of his way, then closed the door behind him as he stepped into the high-ceilinged apartment. She turned to see him pivoting, to take it all in.

He whistled through his teeth. "You live *here?*"

Sibyl managed to say, "I'm house-sitting," in more than a whisper. Barely. When in doubt, give information. "It used to be a warehouse. From the 1800s. You went away."

Wait. That last part wasn't supposed to be out loud.

"Yeah. The others were—" Trace looked at her more closely. Then he ducked and *looked* at her, and his already deep voice roughened. "You look different."

New clothes. New hair. Different makeup. Odd emotions. Sibyl flushed with embarrassment that she hadn't been subtle enough. Now he'd think it was for him. He'd feel sorry for her or, worse, laugh at her....

"The others were what?" she prompted, desperate to distract him.

He didn't laugh. He kept staring at her, even as he said, "The others were going full-steam on that plan they had. You know. The one about redeeming an old society full of rich muckety-mucks?"

"The Comitatus," she proffered, since it was an odd name and so probably hard for him to remember. "Latin for an armed group. Some also cite it as a source for feudalism, an arrangement between the superior and inferior." He winced at that last word. Oh, please, someone stop her. "Would you like a drink?"

"You got beer?"

She shook her head, afraid to open her mouth.

"Anything's good. Anyway—" He followed her to the kitchen. She angled her body so he wouldn't see into her foodless fridge. "Smith and Mitch were all about, 'we can save them,' and I didn't give a crap, so I headed home for a while. Louisiana."

So he hadn't fled her? He just hadn't considered her either way. Maybe he only noticed her when he was rescuing her—or needed information, like today. "Could

you look at something for me, tell me what you think?"
At least she had information.

She got two root beers out of the fridge and turned back, almost bumping into him. His big body seemed to radiate warmth, after the artificial chill. She wanted to lean against him, maybe snuggle closer.

Don't snuggle closer!

"I know," she said, lifting one of the bottles of soda upward in offering. He squinted as he took it, as if momentarily lost in their conversation. "The Comitatus is beyond redemption." Killers. If they hadn't killed her father, why would they have railroaded her for the crime?

"You think so, huh?"

That surprised her. "Don't you think so?"

"I don't think about it." But of course he wouldn't. It was a *secret* society. Every piece of information she'd collected through the years, she'd gotten covertly. And often illegally. "That's kind of why I wanted to talk to you. I need the opinion of someone on the outside. It's easy to know what I'll hear from the guys."

"Not much." So this visit was Comitatus related! "Because the Comitatus take an oath of secrecy when they join, at fifteen."

"Um…yeah. Hey, wanna sit down?"

This was what came of never having visitors. Sibyl felt herself blush as she nodded and headed toward the living area. She jumped, startled, when Trace touched a palm to her back, as if to guide her. To settle her. It might have worked, if he hadn't snatched it away.

"Sorry," he muttered, when she glanced, wide-eyed, over her shoulder.

She shook her head, unsure how to tell him she'd liked it. She hadn't been touched since…the scalp massage, by the hairdresser. And at one point in the last few months, Arden had hugged her—that had been strange. And then when Trace rescued her from the train. Less than three times in three months.

At least the loft's real owner only had settees, not sofas. When she sat on one end, drawing her knees up to her chest, and Trace sank onto the other end, barely a foot of stone-colored suede separated them. She watched how Trace folded himself forward, in an attempt to make his big frame comfortable on the low seat, bracing his elbows on his thighs, clasping his big hands. She wished she knew how to draw, to capture the lines of his rangy body. Her brain wasn't working right.

Especially not when he looked at her again, raised his eyebrows and grinned. Trace had a great grin, like a joke they were in on together. She was supposed to say something, wasn't she? But…if she spoke, then she'd end up answering his questions and he'd go away again. Of course, him leaving would happen either way, but did she have to be the one to launch the visit's end?

"You really do look different," he said again, and she ducked her head, no longer in on the joke. She wanted to run to the bathroom and scrub off the expensive makeup, mess up her hair, go back to Goth eyeliner and nothing else. She wanted to undo the clasp that held some of her hair behind her head, so that it would swing forward and she could hide behind it. Yes, the new look had helped her get into this apartment, far better than most of the places she'd squatted in the past. But that wouldn't matter if he laughed at her.

Then he said, "I like it." And his voice sounded strangled again, and when she peeked back he wasn't looking at her. He was frowning at his big, clasped hands, like *he* felt uncomfortable. Maybe he wasn't making fun of her. No—edit that. This was Trace. Of course he wouldn't make fun of her. He was her hero.

Sibyl risked a smile, though it felt uncertain and new on her lips. "Thank you," she whispered.

Trace slanted a glance back at her, then grinned that between-you-and-me grin again, and Sibyl's insides twisted with unfamiliar, not-quite-comfortable feelings. But as long as Trace was here, she guessed it was safe to feel them.

Still grinning, he leaned forward to where he'd set his long, thick bundle on the glass cocktail table and unfolded the tarp, as if presenting it with a flourish. In shifting his weight forward and then back, he managed to end up closer to her when he sat back. Sibyl liked his wall of warmth. But she followed his lead to look at what he'd brought, so that this new feeling could venture out without the threat of direct attention.

She frowned. "It's a sword." An old, scarred, dusty sword.

"I found it behind the wall of the old LaSalle bungalow," he agreed, raising it by the pommel like a warrior offering his strength and sword to his overlord... right before riding off to conquer peaceful villages, kill menfolk, enslave children and rape women as spoils of war. Sibyl knew his friends had gotten all excited over an ancient Greek sword, back when she'd met them. They called it the sword of Aeneas, and they acted like it was the holy grail. Like it was a sacred relic. A *Comitatus* relic.

Maybe it was. Swords, like guns, had only one purpose—to kill and maim people, maybe to coerce obedience with the threat of killing and maiming. Conquest. Power. And this sword was LaSalle's?

The court finds Isabel Daine guilty of arson and manslaughter.

So much for that new, precious feeling. Now all she felt was nausea. "Put it away."

"But this is what I wanted to ask you about—"

She used her feet to push herself up onto the arm of the settee, leaning as far back from him and his blade as possible. *"Put it away!"*

Trace leaned forward, rewrapped the sword, then sat back.

Well on his end of the settee.

This time, Sibyl didn't have to wonder. He thought she was crazy. Maybe she was. But if so, that was the fault of the Comitatus, of LaSalle, and of whoever had really killed her father. The fault of the kind of men who got excited about weaponry and violence and swords.

That didn't make her heart hurt any less.

Chapter 2

Now Trace had gone and turned her back into a scaredy-cat.

He just hoped she wouldn't faint again.

He wished he knew how much of her problem was the sword, and how much was really him. Little Sibyl had surprised the hell of him. He'd expected to find her staying at some ratty, rent-by-the-week hotel, the kind he and his friends got since quitting their legacies and the Comitatus had left them with cash-only options and little cash. Instead, he found their conspiracy theorist in a glamorous, urban loft. And as for Sibyl herself...?

Trace had thought she was cute before, with her big Bambi eyes and the lithe, ballerina body she hid under oversize clothes. He'd liked how she didn't just talk over *his* head, but the heads of his overly educated friends, which was fun to watch—and which he figured proved her claim that she wasn't a teenager. Nobody got that much education that young. He'd admired her healthy distrust of people, which seemed like its own kind of smart. But at the time, she'd put out such a thick wall of don't-touch-me that he'd more or less kept his distance. He tried to never forget that someone as big as he was could scare people just by saying hello.

Today she'd looked…welcoming. Not just her shiny, clean hair, pulled back to let people see her solemn face, or her nice clothes, though those helped. *Her.*

He could have sworn she was glad to see him, and it had felt great. Trace couldn't remember the last time someone had been honestly glad to see him, except maybe his ma. He couldn't help but want to get closer to her, want to know more.

'Course, Sibyl aimed the exact opposite look at the sword, times ten. Even after he'd wrapped it. What, did she think it would leap out and bite her? Still, she at least sank down to sit on the arm of the loveseat, instead of just using it to brace herself farther away from him. The position made her look taller.

"So, what's with the crazy?" he asked—and she winced. Great job. That would be why he had more weekend flings than regular girlfriends, wouldn't it? Still…was he supposed to ignore this? "It's just a sword."

"It's a *Comitatus* sword." She all but spat the name of his ancestors' secret society.

Cool! Information, just like he'd hoped. "You can tell by looking?"

"No! It's…" She took a deep breath, as if settling

herself. To his relief, she sank back onto the seat cushion, wrapping her arms protectively around her knees. The don't-touch-me-vibes were back with a vengeance. "Reproductions are mostly a twentieth century art form. If the wall was old, this is authentic. No later than eleventh century. Maybe as early as eighth. Dark Ages."

"And you saw all that while you were begging me to put it away."

She scowled at the word *begging,* which was cute, until she said, "Yes."

Okay, then. Even before she rolled her eyes—which she did—Trace saw she thought he was stupid. Compared to her, he probably was, but he didn't like the reminder. Just to be obstinate, he leaned a little closer to her, as if just to listen. He hadn't forgotten his size. He was just… using it.

She smelled good. Like girl. Like a wealthy girl, damn it.

She didn't seem the least bit intimidated. "Cruciform crossguard," she catalogued, as if that meant something…so damn it, maybe he was stupid. Compared to her. That's why he'd come to her, wasn't it? "Double-edged, with only a slight taper, so an earlier than later period. Moderately rounded tip, so more a slashing than a stabbing weapon. Maybe a Viking sword. More likely Gallic." She eyed his expression, then clarified, "French."

"And you know that 'cause…?"

"The five-lobed pommel—that round cap on the end of the grip? Viking invention. Balances the weight. So does the fuller."

He narrowed his eyes. Now she was making up words.

"The fuller is the groove down the center. Roman swords don't have it. So post-Roman Empire. And it's a one-handed sword, to be used with a shield, so pre-High Middle Ages. Also…Vikings. Assimilated by then."

"Vikings aren't French." Trace knew damned well the LaSalle family came from French roots. Hell, most of Louisiana came from French roots. He liked the idea of some French knight wielding the sword in heroic deeds better than he liked descending from Vikings. Weren't Vikings more about murdering and pillaging?

"They're tied to Norman French. Also, true Vikings preferred battle-axes."

Trace chuckled at the image of murdering, pillaging Vikings getting chewed out by big, domineering women.

Sibyl ducked her head and said, "The weapons. Axes. For battle."

"I knew that." And this time, he did. He just liked the other picture better…and he thought he detected a tiny, return smile. Reciting facts seemed to have relaxed Sibyl some, anyway. He felt mean for having leaned closer, but he didn't want to lean away. She didn't seem worried, so he hooked an elbow over the back cushion and stayed where he was. Where he could better smell her. "So it's really old. What else makes it a—a secret society sword?"

"Comitatus," she offered, as if he kept forgetting the word. No wonder she thought he was dumb. But he'd taken a damned oath. That had been the deal. Take his father's name, get his father's money and respectability—join his father's world, including the Comitatus. At the time, he hadn't realized that no amount of money and respectability was worth it. So he'd gone ahead and taken their stupid vow of secrecy.

The least he could do was try not to run around using the society's name.

"Yeah. Them."

"LaSalle." She said his birth-father's surname like something ugly. Since he'd gone by that name for almost ten years, her disgust felt insulting, no matter how he'd come to dislike the Judge. "Why were you in a LaSalle bungalow? Did any Comitatus agents see you take this?"

"I was helping a crew do a gut job on it. You know— taking down the moldy walls, pulling out the ruined insulation before a rebuild." All the God's honest truth. "And no, I didn't see any Comitatus types hanging around. It's pretty dirty work."

She relaxed, and even smiled right at him, like he was someone special just because he did day labor.

"The LaSalle family's big in the New Orleans Comitatus," she explained, and he pretended he didn't know that. "They're a hereditary society. That's how I knew your friends were involved. Donnell. Talbott. Leigh. All hereditary names."

And his illegitimacy had kept him under her radar. "If they're so secret, how would you know…?"

"I'm very smart." Then, to his amazement, she smiled a real, happy smile at him, like she'd said it to tease him instead of to shame him. "And devious."

The smile lit her pretty face and made her beautiful.

It punched him in the gut, how beautiful this maybe wealthy and definitely too-smart-for-him girl was.

So did the sudden, echoing thought of *Mine.*

So did the way he had to act on it. Carefully, damn it.

Suddenly, not scaring her became important again.

Sibyl wasn't sure what changed. One minute Trace was grinning that between-you-and-me grin at her, which she loved. The next—everything shifted, almost imperceptibly and yet seismically at the same time. What happened?

He still smiled, but instead of looking at her, he was…*looking at her.* Searching for something that she wished she knew how to give him. But what did that even mean? Desperate to understand, she tried to catalog the change. His breathing had subtly changed. His pupils dilated, just a little. The air between them felt…hotter. Or maybe it was just *her* breathing and *her* vision and *her* thermoregulation that suddenly fluctuated. Either way, she barely noticed herself dropping her hands to her side instead of clasping her knees between them like a shield.

"So, Smartypants," he said—and the silly name sounded as endearing as Shortstuff had, coming from him. "Are you dating anyone?"

Her? The idea felt ludicrous. She didn't have time to date—secret societies to uncover, anonymity to protect, vengeance to wreak. Having spent her formative years in a girls' penitentiary, among hardened teens who'd practiced unhealthy relationships before their incarcerations, Sibyl wasn't sure she'd know *how* to just date. Why did he want to know? *So, what's with the crazy?*

Was he feeling out just how big a freak she was?

Except…his breath sounded as shallow as hers. They seemed to be sharing this new, shifted reality, just like they'd shared the smile. So, was he actually interested? Had Arden Leigh, mother hen meddler, asked him to find out? Or…?

Unable to analyze the situation further against the deafening rush of her heartbeat in her ears—which she knew was actually just her pulse in her jugular vein or maybe her carotid artery, which were both closer to her ears, and why couldn't she shut her mind off? Unable to manage anything else, Sibyl simply shook her head. Not dating anyone. Not her.

"So…sorry, but I'm kind of distracted, here." Him, too? She'd felt alone for so long, but she wasn't alone in this. Trace leaned closer, his arm over the seatback making him a human wall that would pin her into the leather corner. She didn't mind. She felt her knees falling open, of their own will, to make room for him. "Can I kiss you?"

You mean, may *you kiss me*—thank God she couldn't talk, just now. She nodded a jerky, uncertain nod. Yes. Please.

He moved farther over her, all heat and solidity. She waited and held her breath. She remembered that having a man in her apartment fell under the "Things movies teach you not to do" category, because someone like him could overpower her, and even if she fought back, he'd hurt her, and nobody would hear her screams because these were really high-end apartments with great soundproofing....

But he *wouldn't* overpower her. She realized why he seemed so tense, as he leaned incrementally closer. Why he'd asked first, when she generally thought of him as a man of action instead of words. He was being extra careful of her.

Her hero. Her knight in faded T-shirt. Sweet, silly knight.

So Sibyl strained upward to close the last inch between them and kissed him first.

As soon as she did, she realized her mistake. She pressed her lips to his, which felt surprisingly soft despite the whiskers surrounding them—and then she had no earthly idea what to do next. So she simply smooched him, the kind of kiss someone would press to their mother's cheek, then ducked her forehead against his hard, convenient shoulder. She felt more embarrassed than aroused. Not that she hadn't liked it. But, wasn't kissing one's hero supposed to be more...more....

At least she was breathing. *Oxygen is fuel.* She'd only pretended to faint, that first time they met, after he'd rescued her. She would hate to do it for real.

To her surprise, Trace's fingers wove into her hair, solid and gentle against her scalp, feeling a hundred times better than the shampoo massage at the Galleria. She leaned into the cradle of his palm and risked peeking back up at him.

He wasn't laughing. Or disgusted.

Yes, he was grinning wider now, almost feral—but

still with the intimacy of a shared joke. "Uhm…thanks," he said, his voice more a rasp than a whisper.

Her lips tried to form the words, *You're welcome.* She couldn't seem to put any voice to them. He smelled so good—like real soap and honest work and…and him. The smell that she'd first sampled when he saved her life.

"My turn?" He grinned.

She nodded, desperate not to speak.

So he leaned closer to her. She found herself drawing back from him without meaning to, making him chase her until her shoulders hit the arm of the settee—he wasn't using his hand to direct her head, just supporting it. His smile faded as he *did* follow her down, until he was hovering over her. He held most of his weight off her with one powerful arm, but she felt his jeans slide against her leggings and realized her mistake—she really was trapped—and couldn't seem to mind.

Please, she found herself silently begging. *Please let it be wonderful.*

Then he pressed his lips to hers—didn't just touch them, but pressed, and oh, it was. Wonderful. Could he kiss her? Yes, he *could.*

So very, very well.

Trace's lips didn't feel as soft this time; they felt firm and certain as they framed her lower lip, drawing it into his mouth just the tiniest bit, just enough for him to lick it. That made her shiver. She parted her lips, to give him easier access to that lower one, which suddenly needed a lot more attention. He nipped at it, without actually using his teeth, and sucked on it, and then took advantage of her parted lips to slide that same, intriguing tongue into her mouth….

Thank goodness he was holding her head, because all of Sibyl's skeletal and muscular strength seemed to melt right out of her fingertips and toes. She wasn't thinking anymore, and the silence—silent but for their little gusts of breath, and the sigh of the settee cushions under their shifting weight, and a strangled little mew like a kitten's from somewhere—the silence felt deliciously restful. All she wanted was to open to him—and his solidity and his heat—so she did. She opened her mouth wider against his, flirting her tongue against his, shivering her delight at the sensation. She slid her arms across his broad chest and around his ribs, drawing him closer against her breasts and tummy. Without any instructions, her legs slid around his waist, wide and surprisingly eager, her bare feet hooking behind his knees.

Trace chuckled into her mouth and shifted again, turning with her in his arms so that he lay on his side now and she lay cushioned between him and the seat-back. No longer busy holding his weight off her, his free hand slid over her hip, his fingers flirting across her bottom before sliding up under her oversize shirt. She arched happily against the rough heat of his palm on the bare skin of her back.

Trace broke the seal of their lips to draw his damp mouth up her jaw, his hot breath against her ear as he rasped out, "You good?"

She nodded frantically, bunching handfuls of his T-shirt behind his back, trying to claw her fingers into him. She was very, very good.

"Good." Now he nibbled down her throat, toward her shoulder. She tightened her legs around him, her feet against his hard, wide thighs now. Behind her, his calloused thumb massaged up under her arm, then down across the pillow of her breast and she pressed hard against him. He was pressing pretty hard against her, too. Luckily, she didn't need thought to know what was going on with that. All she needed was animal instinct.

Who would have guessed she'd have so much instinct?

"Hold on," he muttered against her collarbone. She almost whimpered as he slid his hand out of her hair—she'd felt so safe, so precious, with him cradling her like that. But he grasped her hips to hold her as he rolled again, so that he lay on his back and she was straddling him, looking down at his combined hunger and satisfaction. That was okay.

She rolled her hips, savoring the hard press of the denim-constricted bulge that she straddled, and that seemed to make them both very happy. So did his unbuttoning her shirt, surprisingly deft with such big hands, and trailing his fingertips around the outer curve of both breasts.

It felt—wonderful. Primal. Essential. But she flushed and ducked her head, feeling suddenly inadequate. When Trace raised his eyebrows in silent question, she murmured, "I'm not very…"

"C'mere." Now sliding his hands behind her back, he drew her down closer to him and covered one of her breasts with his hot, wet mouth. She heard that strange, kitten-mew again. When he began to apply his tongue, and a little suction, the noise sounded something like a sob. *Her* noise. *Her* sob.

A glorious forever later, he switched to her other poor, neglected breast, covering the first with a callused hand—which more than covered it, him being so big and her being so small—so it wouldn't get too cold. "A mouthful is plenty," he noted, before filling his mouth again.

Sibyl's hands kneaded against the soft cotton covering his chest, feeling the springy sensation of hair beneath the material. She ground herself harder against his crotch. She wanted…she wanted…. Of course she knew what she wanted. Just because she hadn't had sex before didn't make her ignorant. This was the twenty-first century, and she hadn't come of age surrounded by nuns. But she didn't want to have to think, was afraid thinking would get in the way of all this surging sensation, and without thinking she couldn't get to how…or when….

So she just writhed on him and savored it all.

Eventually he was warming the second breast with his thumb, and brushing the curtain of hair back from her face, which freed his mouth for her to kiss him some more. He thrust upward against her, and she liked that, too. No wonder the girls in juvie made such a fuss and stayed with losers for this. But Trace was no loser. At one point, between kisses, he gasped, "Do you want…?"

She nodded. *Yes, yes, yes.* She wanted.

But he didn't do anything other than worship her breasts and watch her face, looking somehow pained, so she kissed him again.

He laughed in the middle of the kiss, though he clearly wasn't laughing at her. "So...?"

So? A cold wash of panic diluted some of the passion flooding through her. He wanted her to make the next move. But she didn't know the next move. Should she undo his jeans? That would mean scooting back off his searing heat and hardness, which she didn't want to do. Trying to take off his shirt would mean moving, too, and letting him stop touching her. She liked it better when he was making the decisions about this.

Trace waited.

"You do it," she pleaded, and his brows drew together in confusion.

Increasingly frustrated, she defaulted to the cruder, clearer words most of the girls in lockdown used. "Do me."

But his mixture of confusion and—disappointment? That stopped her. So did the way his hands stilled against her temple, against her breast.

"What?" he challenged, and now he sounded... angry? And she didn't know why. Not that men seemed to need a reason to be angry with her, but...she'd liked him being different.

Okay, he really wanted her to do it? She reluctantly scooted back on his thighs, so that she could better reach his jeans. She struggled with the metal button at the top of the closing, and Trace drew a deep, shaking breath, his eyes falling shut.

She used that moment to take a deep breath herself, and studied the zipper. Zippers were about as easy as it came, except his was really straining against the erection beneath it, and she didn't want to hurt him, and maybe she should slide her hand into his pants, between him and the zipper, to protect him, except she wasn't sure there was room, and…

She looked back up at him, and he was waiting with the oddest expression on his face.

"I don't…" But she couldn't admit she didn't know how. She just couldn't. Knowing things was her only real talent, the only reason he'd come here. "*You* do it."

Trace groaned and rocked forward. He caught her under her arms with both hands, lifted her easily. The next thing she knew, he'd leaned her against the suede arm at the opposite end of the settee and was looming in over her, and she felt a little scared of what would happen but she felt a lot more relieved than frightened because she knew, *knew* he wouldn't hurt her, and she wanted it to be him—

And then, instead of kissing her the way they'd been kissing since this started, he gave her an odd, closed-mouth smooch on her cheek. Then he drew back.

He waited, scowling. And breathing hard. His eyes were still dilated. He clearly still wanted this. So why…?

Confused, Sibyl reached for him—but he spread a hand against her naked chest, just under her throat, and held her at arm's length. Trace Beaudry had pretty long, thick arms. When she tried to reach for him again, he didn't give an inch.

"How many guys have you been with?" he demanded.

She shook her head.

"C'mon, Smartypants. How many have you *done?*"

"None!" There. She'd said it.

But Trace let loose a few crude terms of his own, in a completely different context, and slumped back against his end of the seat. When Sibyl tried to follow, he said, *"No!"*

So she stayed where she was. She buttoned her shirt and felt humiliated.

"What, you thought I didn't need to know? Or maybe I'd get stupid?" He was still scowling when she peeked back up from her buttons. "It's not like I have money anymore."

She still couldn't think, so she didn't say anything. She felt like crying from the rejection and the confusion and the dissatisfied ache. He was looking at her like the freak she was now. She wanted to explain that she hadn't known it would upset him. She wanted to tell him that to get sex before she turned eighteen, she would have had to go with girls or guards—like clarifying *that* would recommend her. She wanted to cite studies about approximate age at first intercourse, and how being among about 10 percent of Americans who'd waited, while a minority, didn't exactly make her as unusual as Bigfoot sightings or unicorns, either.

And damn it, once she started thinking in statistics, the moment—and that blessed, blissful silence—was pretty much gone.

Most of all, she wanted to be back in his arms, no matter what he was doing to her while there. She'd felt… she'd felt….

But feelings weren't Sibyl's forte.

Trace scrubbed a splayed hand down his face, then

looked at her over it. "Don't give me those big Bambi eyes. I'm the one you just…who's still…."

But whatever he'd meant to say, he deleted. He didn't look quite as angry.

Don't cry. Don't cry. Don't cry. "Faline," whispered Sibyl finally.

"What?" She didn't think he meant to snap the way he did.

She took a deep, shaking breath. "Bambi was a boy-deer. Faline was the girl-deer."

She hadn't meant it as a joke, but his bark of laughter still eased her distress. He wasn't too angry to laugh, anyway. "Fine. Don't give me those big, *Faline* eyes." He searched her face. "So this really wasn't some kind of plot to get my father's money?"

She shook her head against visions of rags-to-riches lottery winners. "Your father has money?"

"Ex-father. It's a long…crap. Look, I'm sorry if I overreacted." Now he reached across the space between them to catch some of her hair between his fingers, to tuck it behind her ear. She let him, savored his touch. "You mean you really wanted me for your first time? Just…*me?*"

As opposed to…? Warily, Sibyl nodded. "Why wouldn't I?"

"'Cause I'm just some illegitimate good ol' boy who grew up in a trailer park on the wrong side of the tracks." He said it like that was supposed to scare her off. "I don't even have a job right now."

And I'm an ex-con. And I'm so broken, I never even looked at a man until you. And the guy who owns this apartment doesn't know I'm house-sitting, which kind of makes us trespassers. Did Trace really think *he* wasn't good enough for *her?* Sibyl shrugged, even attempted a smile and a joke. "At least you aren't Comitatus."

His expression…stilled. A momentary pause in his breathing. A flicker of guilt in his eyes. Nothing more. "Yeah," he said, but he sounded uncomfortable saying it—and then she knew. Because, whether she wanted to be or not, she was very, *very* smart.

Smart enough to rearrange seemingly unconnected tidbits of data into a new, unmistakable pattern.

When she'd met Trace, he was with three Comitatus descendents.

His father—ex-father?—was apparently wealthy.

If illegitimate, he might not bear his birth father's name.

"You are Comitatus," she accused in a whisper. This time she *wanted* him to laugh at her. She wanted him to deny it, maybe more than she'd ever wanted anything except for the nightmare of her father's death, of her wrongful imprisonment, to never have happened. But he didn't deny it. He opened, then closed his mouth. He swallowed, tried again, but only managed, "How…?"

By then, new and worse patterns had revealed themselves.

He'd brought her a sword from the LaSalle house. How had he happened to end up gutting the LaSalle house?

He had a cleft chin. By genomic imprinting, that could only be inherited from one's father. She'd seen a chin like that before. And the pale eyes in his dark face, the same color as….

The court finds Isabel Daine guilty…

Sibyl stood. "Excuse me."

"Wait."

But she kept walking toward the bathroom, unwilling to show weakness, unable to show anything. She concentrated on taking one step after another, the ache in her throat tightening, tightening. "Are you okay?"

Sibyl made herself look over her shoulder toward where Trace now stood, looking concerned. She made herself smile to show teeth. "I'm fine," she lied. As a child, she'd never lied. Jail—and the Comitatus—had turned her into this.

Then she locked the bathroom door behind her. She turned on the overhead fan. She turned on the water.

Then she fell to her knees and vomited, violently but almost silently, into the toilet.

She'd almost slept with the bastard son of Judge René LaSalle.

Chapter 3

Beckett Covington, intern for attorney Dillon Charles, liked to multitask. MP3 player, check. Texting with one hand, check. Because if all he had to do was stare at his laptop screen, skimming the assigned thumbnail images and hitting the page-down key every few seconds, he'd lose it from boredom. He'd known this job would include scut work, but damn. Eyeballing almost five hundred shots of manual laborers, taken at the site of an old house nobody had lived in for decades?

Still, Dillon Charles wasn't just Beckett's boss, but his superior within the rankings of the great and powerful Comitatus. Just like the Judge was Charles's superior. So it had been for centuries, and so it was this afternoon. Although a few centuries ago, squires probably got more interesting tasks than—

Wait. Now, when his phone beeped, Beckett texted "BRB" and put it down.

He paged back up on the laptop, maximized an image and leaned closer. One of the construction crew working on LaSalle's bungalow looked damned familiar. Could that possibly be…?

Doing *construction?* God, the Judge would be mortified.

Beckett printed the picture, then began reviewing the others with renewed interest. This time he was searching for a particular height, a particular color of shirt…a particular scandal. He printed more pertinent shots. He even ditched the iPod. Maybe interning didn't suck so badly, at that.

Up-and-coming attorney Dillon Charles was about to go on the warpath.

And Beckett hoped he got to see it.

Sibyl huddled on the travertine tile, her face in her hands and her elbows on the toilet seat. How could she have been so blind?

"You don't know for sure," she whispered to herself, then argued back with an almost voiceless, "So ask."

But she didn't want to. "Because you already know the answer."

Stop talking to yourself. The habit had begun in self-preservation, back in juvie. Even predators who went after small, underaged girls generally gave crazy people a wide berth. By the time of Sibyl's parole, it was harder to stop than she would have thought, especially under stress.

She jumped when Trace hammered on the bathroom door and called, "It's not like it matters." He sounded especially loud and real, in contrast to her whispers. "Even if I did once join some stupid society—not, you know, that I'm saying I did—I quit. Would have quit. If I belonged. Crap!"

The way he fumbled around the oath of secrecy he'd surely taken only exacerbated her shame. She'd missed this? That the Comitatus had ever trusted him with privileged information….

Privileged information. Like, maybe, who killed her father?

Sibyl stood—unsteadily, but she stood.

"Look, you're kind of scaring me here," Trace called. "You want me to leave, I'll leave, but let me know you're okay. Okay?"

The Comitatus had entrusted Trace with privileged information. He'd since quit them. He referred to LaSalle as his *ex*-father. And he liked her. At least, he'd kissed her as if he liked her, hadn't he? From what little she knew of kissing?

He hammered on the door again, rattling it in its frame. "Sibyl? Just say something!" More hammering. If they weren't careful, the neighbors would call the police, soundproofing or not. The police would call the apartment's real owner, on his extended business trip. The real owner would ask, what house-sitter?

"I'm okay," she called, and flushed the toilet. He stopped pummeling the door. Quickly, she lit a scented candle, then began rinsing her mouth. What if…? She felt guilty to consider it, but she shouldn't! She'd been searching for a chink in René LaSalle's armor for years. Now, just outside that door, stood proof of the Judge's fallibility. And he cared about her. Sort of. Maybe.

What if this was an opportunity?

Sibyl wondered how far she would go to bring the Comitatus down. Could she kiss Trace again, knowing his lips were LaSalle lips? Could she welcome his hands against her bare skin again, open her legs for him? Surely not! But she didn't have to go that far, did she? She could blame virginal timidity.

Straightening, drying her hands, she stared at herself one more time in the mirror. Her hair had come down, but it made a better shield that way. Her color looked off, but otherwise, her expression was a mask.

"For Daddy," she and her reflection whispered to each other.

Then she heard the apartment door close.

By the time she'd leaned into the hallway, Trace had gone. He'd taken his sword and his secrets with him. And she couldn't tell if she was relieved or not.

"Holy guacamole, Trace—it's gorgeous!"

"When were you going to tell us about this?"

Just as Trace had figured, his fellow outcasts—Mitch Talbott and Smith Donnell, in that order—appreciated the sword a lot more than Sibyl had. Their eyes caressed it where it lay on the dining room table.

"I'm telling you now," Trace snapped, at Smith's criticism. "Sibyl says it's…" He concentrated. "Eighth– to eleventh–century. Because of Vikings and using one hand and a bunch of other stuff I wouldn't have thought about."

"You took it to Conspiracy Girl before you brought it to us?" The brown-haired Texan, Smith, had built his own security business with help from Trace, Mitch and another friend from college. He'd lost the business after their exile, of course. But sometimes he still acted like everyone's boss.

Trace folded his arms, lifted his chin and narrowed his eyes down at the others. "Yeah. I took it to her before I brought it to you."

Trace expected more questions. He sure as hell had some! Instead, the guys just went back to the sword. Blond Mitch, who kind of resembled a surfer dude, crouched by the ornate table to get an eye-level view. Smith leaned over it, hands spread as if to guesstimate its length against his own Comitatus blade. "Don't y'all want to know how she's doing?"

Smith said nothing, but Mitch shrugged. "Nah. We see her once or twice a week."

Really? "I thought she hated you two. 'Cause you're Comitatus." Or maybe she only hated him for that.

Smith barely looked up. "Oh, she hates us all right."

"Her hatred makes me sad inside," agreed Mitch—but with his usual grin. "I have no idea why someone who hates secret societies would become such an expert on them…unless it's like an epidemiologist. Epidemics aren't fun either. She likes Greta, though. And Dido." Their landlady's cocker spaniel ran in a happy circle at the sound of her name. She still hadn't recovered from the excitement of Trace's return. "Sometimes she comes by on the days Greta's teaching piano at Arden's rec center. They put a leash on the dog and Sibyl walks both of them."

"You know that I can hear you," chided Greta from the large pantry. "It's my eyes that are going, not my ears."

"Just checking." Mitch laughed, widening his eyes in feigned guilt.

Trace had somehow expected more to change, after he'd left. "So you two are still staying here? Nobody's bothered the place?"

"Nah. Smith's been staying in Highland Park with his giiirl frieeend, now that her brother's back in school. But they come here to slum with us pretty much daily, 'cause of the rec center. And as long as Greta's willing to have me, I'm just happy to stay someplace that doesn't smell like feet. Especially since Smith's deal with the local Schmomitatus still stands."

That was Mitch's playful way around their vow of secrecy—speak instead about a hypothetical society called the Schmomitatus. It's not like they felt too much need to stay stealthy around Greta. Her own father had rebelled against the society decades ago, a fact she learned herself when he'd developed late onset dementia and began talking. The fact that she was "of the blood" had, at Smith's insistence, won asylum for her old Victorian home on the bad side of town and everything in a five-block radius. That included the light-rail stop and Arden's recreation center for teenaged girls.

"I'm the one who's happy to have you." Greta reappeared from the pantry with several cans of sauerkraut. She looked old and German and deceptively frail. "You'll stay here, too, Trace."

"Yes, ma'am," he said. "So Sibyl—she's doing okay, then?"

"Why?" asked Smith. "Did she pull a Sibyl while you were talking with her? You know, turn around and walk off in the middle of a conversation without saying anything?"

No, she said "Excuse me." But her voice had sounded so…strained.

"Jump at nothing?" suggested Mitch. "She's so damned serious you forget, and then *bam!* Skittish as a deer."

Faline, thought Trace, and scowled.

"Did she explain how Elvis is still alive?" tried Smith.

"Actually, she doesn't say he's alive," Mitch laughed. "She thinks he faked his death, but that it doesn't grant the man immortality."

"You boys be nice," chided Greta from the stove, less affection in her tone this time. "Not everyone gets to grow up safe and well off. Yes, Trace, Sibyl is doing fine. Some personal damage just takes longer to heal."

Smith and Mitch had the good grace to look ashamed. Honestly so, even.

Trace growled, "Who damaged her?"

Other than me?

"That's none of our business. But she's got us now. She's being social—something she seems rather new at—spending time with me, and at the rec center with

Arden and Valeria. Even arguing with you boys. It's all good for her. Let her move at her own speed."

Would that be the speed that had her wrapping her legs around his waist and inhaling his tongue into her mouth? Or the speed of someone with big, frightened eyes who didn't know how to free a guy from his jeans? Damn, Sibyl didn't need someone as clumsy and stupid as Trace. Not if she was damaged. She needed…she needed…

But Trace couldn't imagine trying to pair her off with anyone else, not even Mitch who, despite all his jokes, was maybe the nicest guy he knew. The mere thought of it made him want to smash nice guy Mitch senseless.

Mine.

Crap.

And now his friends were staring at him, confused— and, in Mitch's case, kinda worried. Time to change the subject.

"So you think the sword's Com—" Trace stopped himself, cursing the day he'd ever thought joining his wealthy father's hereditary secret society was a good idea. Greta was listening.

Mitch cleared his throat. "*Schmomi*tatus."

"—yeah, that it's one of their swords?"

Smith said, "You know? If we knew more about the connection between swords and the society, we might be able to figure that out."

"So, tell me, tough girls," asked Val Diaz's voice, from the large meeting room across the hallway from the computer "lab" where Sibyl worked. Labored, anyway.

Between her low overhead—squatters don't pay rent—and her need to "stay off the grid," she didn't keep a steady job. Someone with her computer genius could always find short, well paying projects when needed. "Some wannabe gangsta grabs you from behind—like this!"

One of the girls let out a squeak, so Sibyl assumed Val had acted out the attack.

"What do you do, huh? Tell me your options!"

Sibyl hesitated and cocked her head, her fingers hovering over the keyboard. She hadn't come to Arden Leigh's rec center to eavesdrop on a self-defense-for-women lecture. She'd come to wipe and reconfigure the hard drives on a batch of used, donated computers.

Yes, her. Doing favors. For the daughter of a Comitatus leader.

But Sibyl figured, if Arden let her work on the computers at the center, maybe next she'd ask Sibyl to help with her computers at her house. Her house where her late father had conducted so much of his Comitatus business. That information on *those* hard drives could be a gold mine. Somewhere, someday, Sibyl *would* find what she needed to understand her father's death, her own life's ruin.

And in the meantime? Sibyl kind of liked it here.

In answer to Val's question, a girl called, "Shoot the bastard!" The others laughed.

"Stupid," whispered Sibyl to herself.

"Uh-huh," drawled the unseen Val, making it sound like a synonym for *stupid,* which almost made Sibyl smile. "Where've you got the gun? Up your sleeve? I didn't think so. Also, it's illegal, 'cause y'all are too young for a carry license. Also? This neighborhood sees too much collateral damage as it is."

Sibyl glanced at the five donated computers, all of which were slowly reformatting large-capacity hard drives. It's not like she had anything to do in here for a while, other than torture herself for not having followed up on the opportunity that was Trace Beaudry-LaSalle. Curious, she drifted across the bright-yellow hall while another girl asked, "What's collateral damage?"

"Accidentally killing a two-year-old bystander instead of the scum-sucker you meant to shoot, that's what." Val Diaz stood with her forearm loosely across the neck of one of the teenagers. Of the half dozen high school girls clustered around her, most of them already stood taller than Sibyl. Many had more curves, too.

No wonder Trace had pushed her away when he'd learned she was a virgin. She'd probably made him feel like a pedophile.

"So what else can you do?" Val couldn't look less like her socialite business partner. Yes, she and Arden both overshadowed Sibyl. But Val came from this troubled South Oak Cliff neighborhood, not Arden's posh Highland Park. Val stood taller, sturdier, more athletic, with tied back, kinky brown hair and tawny skin and cheekbones like a stone idol's. *Mestizo,* thought Sibyl.

Val regarded the girls drily. "Seriously? None of you has a better solution? You'll just pass out?"

"Turn your head into the crook of his elbow." The suggestion surprised Sibyl more than anyone, because she was the one who made it. Loud enough to be heard, even. Worse, now everyone in the small gymnasium turned to look at her.

"Thanks, Sib," called Val, who'd certainly seen her around. Around here, and around Trace, Mitch and Smith. "Tell them why the crook of the elbow."

"Relieves the pressure on the trachea." Noting several blank looks, Sibyl clarified, "You can breathe."

"Good. What then?" Releasing her original guinea pig, Val beckoned to her.

Since everyone stared anyway, Sibyl sidled closer. "Yell." For allies. For guards. For anyone. It wasn't like pride had any place in self-defense.

Several of the teens laughed. But one of them, a black girl with loop earrings and gorgeous fingernails, asked, "What if nobody can hear you?"

"Yell anyway. Gets you breathing." Oxygen is fuel.

"What then?" Val held out one arm, eyebrows raised in a silent request. Or demand. Val was kind of alpha. In this, she vaguely reminded Sibyl of a fellow juvenile inmate named Wanda, the hulking drug dealer who'd taught her all this back in lockup. Sibyl had come to count on Wanda, marginally. That was *almost* trust.

Val was also the only person among Sibyl's Dallas companions who had no ties to the Comitatus, other than Tra—

No. Val was the only one.

Sibyl stepped closer and pivoted, allowing the taller woman to put her into a loose headlock. She turned her throat into the crook of Val's elbow. It almost felt like an embrace. "Then you bargain."

"Bargaining is for wimps," complained a skinny white girl with tight brown cornrows. "I'd kick his ass."

"If enough of her friends are surrounding you, you can't." Sibyl noticed that Val loosened her hold even further, and realized what she'd said. "*His* friends."

Bargaining was all that had saved her. Not *begging*— *please* just made predators laugh. But offering something? *I'm smart. I can help you get out of here.* She'd almost passed out by then, because she was so frightened. She'd only been twelve. She hadn't learned the turn-your-head trick yet. *I can help you get your GED.*

Wanda had let go and challenged Sibyl to earn her safety by doing just that. When a combination of tutoring and cheating got Wanda that degree, they moved on to get her an associates, and Sibyl got the protection of the toughest girls in the facility. Sibyl didn't have to imagine what would have happened otherwise; she'd seen it happen to others. She'd hated watching, afraid and unable to help. She'd cried at night, from the guilt.

Maybe today, she could help just a little. "But if he's alone, grab his pinkie finger and yank." She illustrated the grab, if not the yank. "Even someone as little as I am can break a pinkie finger."

"Good." But something about Val's tone had changed, like she was talking more to Sibyl than to the class, now. Almost gentle. "What else?"

"If you're wearing shoes, scrape your heel down his shin."

"That would hurt like hell," Val agreed. "What else?"

"Once he lets you go—from the pain—slam the heel of your hand into his nose." Sibyl turned out of Val's loose grip to demonstrate. "Or clap your hands onto both his ears at once. Or pretend you're going along with it, caress his face, then gouge his eyes out with your thumbs."

The teens broke into a chorus of *"ew!"* Because eyeball goo was worse than being attacked or killed? Sibyl and Val exchanged dry looks at their disgust, like they were friends or something. But they weren't friends. Sibyl didn't have friends. She couldn't.

She backed away from the older woman. "I…computers."

Then, leaving Val with the teens, she hurried back to her original room. The computers still had a way to go before she could reinstall operating systems, but she preferred privacy. That had been…that had…

She shook her head. Arden and Val had taken it upon themselves to try to improve the teens' lives, but Sibyl hadn't. She couldn't lose focus on her own mission. *Defeat the Comitatus.* No matter what.

Across the hall, she heard Val asking, "So what do you do if nothing works? He's overpowered you, or his friends are there, and you're out of options. I hope this never happens, but y'all need to consider it. Do you fight, and maybe die, or do you give up, and maybe live? What do you do?"

The chorus of replies tangled together, so that Sibyl didn't have to imagine which of the faces she'd just memorized was offering what possibility. She didn't want to know. She didn't want to calculate the odds, already factoring in details like the cast on one girl's wrist, or the extra foundation another wore, like it could cover a bruise. These girls weren't her responsibility, any more than the ones who'd screamed for help in front of her, not so many years ago....

"You survive," she whispered to herself, answering Val anyway. "You survive, so that you can come back and destroy them. Destroy everything they love. Burn their lands, salt their fields and erase all memory of them."

She'd developed a plan, damn it. Get close to Trace. Milk him for information about his birth father. Use it against the Comitatus who'd killed her own father, ruined her mother, stolen her life. All she had to do, to start was...see him again.

See him, and make him think she liked him. But not really like him. Because that way only lay pain.

Staring sightlessly at the blue bars on the churning CPUs, Sibyl hugged herself. She tried to feel better with her plan.

She felt very alone, instead.

Beckett Covington rolled his shoulders, trying to get control of his excitement. Before he walked through the mahogany door, into his boss's office, he had to compose himself. Yes, he'd kicked butt on this assignment. Yes, Mr. Charles would undoubtedly be pleased. But if he wanted to advance in this society, Beckett had to play this off as business-as-usual.

One more deep breath and—there. Professional.

He knocked on the door and, at the call to enter, pushed through with the hand not holding the folder.

"I've found him, sir. He's in Dallas, with two other exiles."

Chapter 4

Trace had to spit nails—literally—to protest, "Greta, wait! Let me get it."

"Nonsense," chided his elderly landlady, continuing blithely in the direction of the front door. "You're busy putting up the wainscoting."

Trace dropped a still-unattached chair rail and ploughed across the dining room, barely dodging the barking dog, to completely block her path. "You're an old blind lady harboring Schmomitatus exiles on the bad side of town. I'll get it."

Greta seemed immune to his size and scary growl of command, damn it. She said something about having been born here, as if South Oak Cliff was the same garden spot it had been so long, long, long ago. Trace glanced out the diamond-paned glass to preview their visitor—something Greta and her bad vision couldn't do anymore—and stopped listening. Bad guys would have been simpler.

Sibyl. After a week of silence, Sibyl had returned.

She stood on the front porch, staring solemnly downward instead of scanning her peripheral like most sane women would. Apparently, she hadn't noticed the kind of neighborhood Greta lived in either.

Trace yanked open the door. "You came here alone?"

He caught her by the shoulder and swept her easily inside, shutting and locking the door behind her as if they were under siege. Okay, so he was overreacting. They hadn't been under siege for months. But damn! There she stood, looking small and vulnerable with too much sexy, bare leg showing between her short skirt and her cowboy boots…kind of a white trash look that just endeared her to him more, like he needed her kind of trouble. Only her green fleece hoodie acknowledged that it was mid-freaking-November already. Did she have no sense of self-preservation at all?

Considering that she'd almost slept with him? Probably not. But she'd shut him out afterward, so maybe. *Complicated* didn't begin to explain her.

Now she looked up at him with those big, brown Faline eyes, and he wished he could tell if she was happy, or angry, or even bored to see him again. In return, he did his impression of a rock. A sweaty, sawdust-smeared rock.

Then Greta said, "Sibyl! How nice to see you again." In unison, Sibyl and Trace looked at her. The awkward moment passed.

Except that Trace should probably let go of her shoulder, now. So he did.

"Hello, Greta." Even that basic a greeting sounded measured, from the Shortstuff. Her "Hello, Dido," came more easily as she sank into a crouch to catch the happy, spinning dog into an embrace. Trace watched how she relaxed into the animal's affection. He noticed how the move showed off her bare knees, how her skirt bunched between her legs as she glanced back up at him with her old mask. "Trace."

"So I come after the dog? Great." Only when he saw the hint of a smile fade from her expression did he realize it even had been there, and maybe not all for Dido after all. He could read Greta's grandmotherly disappoval more clearly.

Yeah. He was a ladies' man, all right. Figuring he couldn't make things worse—in the next few seconds, anyway—he offered a hand to help Sibyl back up, by way of apology.

With one last kiss for Dido—lucky dog—she gave hers. Trace liked the feel of her cool, slim hand in his and held on to it a moment longer than necessary after she stood, beautifully balanced, not needing his help at all.

"I've made gingerbread, dear," offered Greta. "Would you like some?"

Sibyl looked from Greta to Trace, as if confused.

"I'd like some," he admitted, and Sibyl nodded. Belatedly she added, "Thank you." To one of them. He couldn't tell which. He hated feeling stupid.

Moments later they sat at Greta's old kitchen table

with frosted gingerbread squares and two glasses of milk, and all Trace could notice was Sibyl's knee touching his thigh under the table. *Damn.* "I called you," he accused. Just in case she hadn't gotten the message he'd recorded. *Sorry it got weird. You okay?*

She nodded, taking a delicate bite of the cake.

Trace wanted to point out that she hadn't called him back, but she probably knew that. Also? He'd been kind of relieved not to hear from her. As much as she fascinated him, as surely as she aroused his protective instincts, as amazing as she'd felt in his arms—and under his hands and his mouth—he didn't need to get involved with someone as delicate and educated and freaking confusing as her.

Also? Trace wasn't a girl. No return call? Message received.

He took his own bite of sugary goodness—damn, but Greta could bake! —and so had his mouth full when Sibyl suddenly looked back up at him.

"I like you," she announced gravely. "I don't like that you're a LaSalle—"

She knew he was—? "I'm not a LaSalle," he corrected sharply. "Not anymore. I'm a Beaudry."

"And I like you."

He stopped chewing and studied her. Sibyl scowled quickly back down at the slice of gingerbread in front of her. He looked at Greta, who raised an eyebrow before turning back to the refrigerator. He looked back at Sibyl, who radiated tension. Ladies man, Trace was not. But even he knew those words shouldn't sound so forced.

Then again, she already knew he was poor. She knew

he was Comitatus. Why else would she say it, unless she meant it? She'd seemed to like him back in her loft, before it all went to hell. He swallowed the gingerbread, then grinned despite himself. "Really?"

She slanted her gaze back up at him, and her wariness eased into incredulity. She even started to smile back before she abruptly looked away and nodded. So—she liked him, but didn't want to? She didn't like him, but said she did because…why? She liked him but wasn't sure how to convey it?

That last one seemed downright cute, and it made the most sense. Especially with the whole virgin business, which seriously scared the crap out of him. The one time he'd slept with a virgin, he'd been a virgin, too, and the whole thing had been clumsy and embarrassing for them both. On the plus side, it had still been sex. And he'd gotten significantly better in the decade since.

Slowing down for the note-passing, head-ducking, hand-holding crap? He'd lost all chance at that since he turned fifteen and got sucked into a world of far more sophisticated girls. But those women were in his past now. And Sibyl…well, she intrigued him. And he had to say something.

"Thanks. You don't suck yourself."

When she looked back up—no dodging his gaze this time—her eyes had widened in disbelief at him. He bumped her knee with his thigh, under the table, grinning wider. "Got you to look."

Her mouth opened, then closed. Hah—Miss Vocabulary had no words? Lesson One, Smartypants: liking someone has nothing to do with words, especially on the guy's part.

He nudged her knee again. This time she took up the unspoken challenge and nudged his thigh back. So he swung his booted foot around to catch her delicate, leather-protected ankle. She slung her free foot around to pin his ankle between both of hers, still under the table. Foot hug. Over the table, he reached around her to tickle her in the ribs, on her off side—that's how small she was compared to him. When she twisted away from his attack with a yelp—a laughing yelp, thank goodness—she started to fall off her chair but ended up right against his side, soft and warm in the nook under his arm, just where he'd wanted her.

To his surprise, he really did want her there.

"I win," he growled softly down at her. And the bright, unguarded smile she turned up at him... He could hardly breathe around the sudden lump of fear in his gut. Because the smile turned her slender face from pretty to downright gorgeous. And the weight of her smiling only at him...

It almost convinced him that he wouldn't screw this up royally. Almost.

Greta cleared her throat. Sibyl flushed, then straightened. Trace just grinned at the old woman because, abruptly, he felt like grinning at everyone. Sibyl liked him. Not Smith Donnell of the Fort Worth Donnells. Not Mitch Talbott of the Lauderdale Talbotts. *Him*. She'd smiled just for him.

"If you spill that milk, you're cleaning it," warned Greta.

"Yes, ma'am," said Trace, and winked at Sibyl.

"Yes, ma'am," said Sibyl, ducking her head again. But her avoiding his gaze didn't worry Trace as much as it had, a few minutes earlier.

Bad idea or not, lousy timing or not, he felt flattered as hell. Sibyl liked him.

Pretending to like Trace proved both easier and more difficult than Sibyl had theorized. Yes, he represented the best chance she might get to learn about Judge LaSalle, possibly to uncover secrets darker than a bastard son. And yes, her greatest fear, that she couldn't convince him, had proved irrelevant. But she hadn't factored in the possibility that her affection might threaten to become more than an act.

Trace really was the birth son of her greatest known enemy. In the last week, she'd obtained pictures from the Judge's youth. She'd been able to see similarities in Trace's eyes. Nose. Jaw. She could see the resemblance in the genomic imprinting of his cleft chin. But now that she'd mustered the courage to face him again, he'd looked nothing like the Judge and a hundred percent like Trace. And he'd grinned at her. And he'd touched her. Offered his hand. Pressed his leg against hers. Tickled her ribs.

She liked being touched. She liked not feeling so isolated in her own body.

He's your enemy.

But he was also her best source. Maybe LaSalle's greatest weakness.

She only had two choices. One? Stay away from

Trace and risk never learning enough to bring the Judge and his cohorts down. Or two? Risk getting close to Trace and pump him for information. She'd hungered for revenge far longer than she'd hungered for anything as pedestrian as human touch.

That first afternoon, after they finished their gingerbread, she helped him with his home improvement project and used what information—dependable, nonthreatening information—she'd collected about ninth-century French swords to start the sharing process.

It got her talking again, anyway. Providing information proved much easier than sharing anything about herself.

"The sword could be Charlemagne's," she admitted, holding a piece of molding that Trace called a chair rail against the wall, just under waist height, as he secured it with small nails. He needed only one blow each. *Wham!* But just as the violence of the hammer began to frighten her, he guided her gently sideways, toward the half he'd secured, so that he could continue on her other side. The contrast unnerved her. "He's a heroic French conqueror and epic hero. Other epic heroes of the period include Roland, of course, and Girard de Roussillon, Aymeri de Narbonne, or even Saint William of Gellone."

She tried not to notice the way the soft fabric of Trace's T-shirt strained against the breadth of his shoulders. Noticing such things hardly helped her concentration.

Trace snorted through the nails in his mouth and said, muffled, "You think a sword like that belonged to a saint and not a warrior?"

"William—Guillaume, in French—was sainted for killing Muslims," Sibyl clarified. "The ancient Comitatus was all about conquering and killing."

Trace continued to secure the nails—*whap!*—without commenting.

"Did they tell you that, before you joined?" she continued, as he finished with that length of chair rail. Trace looked guilty when he glanced at her. Because he took vows of secrecy, she reminded herself. "They had to tell you something, before you took vows."

Trace shrugged and picked up another length of molding. One-handed. "So who's this guy you're house-sitting for?"

Wham!

He changed topics as subtlely as he pounded nails.

She reminded herself that she wouldn't learn all his secrets in one afternoon. So she lied about her fictional house-sitting job, and he told her a little bit about his "Ma's" bed-and-breakfast in Stagwater, Louisiana, and she felt satisfaction at the afternoon's progress. Before he would ever get to the good stuff about his dad, he had to trust her, right? She let him walk her back to the light-rail station, despite not feeling particularly at risk on the "poor side of town." He didn't hold her hand, or put his arm around her. She wasn't wholly sure what was normal, and didn't want to show her ignorance, so she didn't reach for him either. She surreptitiously watched how he scanned their surroundings as they walked, like a predator on the prowl, simultaneously hunting both prey and rivals. Even the gangbangers gave him wide berth. She wondered what he did on the rare occasion that a rival, in size or toughness, actually appeared.

Only as they hiked across the parking lot to the West-moreland DART station, hearing the distant whistle of the northbound train's approach, did he clear his throat and say, "Let me know when you're coming back. I'll meet the train."

"That's stupid. I can—" But something about the way his expression darkened clued her in to her near misstep. He had a ferocious scowl. The expression reminded her that he could probably break her neck with one hand. He wouldn't, LaSalle blood or not. She felt sure. But still…

"I don't like talking on the phone," she confessed instead, and felt her cheeks flush despite the nip in the air. Because it was the truth. The Comitatus couldn't know what had happened to "Isabel Daine" after her parole—unless they'd tapped her mother's phone out in Oregon or wherever she'd moved after remarrying. Sibyl didn't want to involve her mother, anyway. And she had nobody else. But how had she become the one parting with secrets now?

He shrugged. "So one-ring me, and I'll head this way." No questions. No judgment. Just that simple a solution.

Before she could stop to think—she didn't dare think—Sibyl hugged him. Her hands couldn't meet behind him, but her head tucked perfectly against his thrumming heart under his flannel shirt. Belatedly, his arms wrapped her thoroughly in return, hard and warm, and his head tipped down over her. His body and sawdust scent surrounded her. No escape. Why wasn't she more frightened?

"So you'll call?" he demanded toward her hair, and it took her far too long to remember what they were talking about. She'd gotten distracted by how she'd begun to equate his scent with safety.

She nodded, rubbing her cheek against his shirted chest like a cat before she pulled back and ran for the train.

She wanted to wear his smell back to the loft.

That couldn't be good.

The next time she went to see him, two days later, she did as he asked. She dialed his number, let it ring once, then disconnected. Sure enough, when she stepped off the train onto the wet, windy platform, there he stood, arms folded. He wore a wrinkled canvas field coat, blue jeans, work boots and a scowl. His scowl eased when he spotted her. He raised his eyebrows at her instead of waving, clearly aware that she couldn't help but notice him towering over the rest of the public.

"Mitch loaned me the car," he said as she reached him, and he hustled her to another of his friend's primer-colored works-in-progress. He touched her jacketed back to guide her, opening the passenger door for her. She slid onto the duct-tape-patched vinyl bench seat and pulled the door shut against the November rain. In contrast to the cold, the car smelled of age, and warmth—and the faint scent of Trace, even before he swung into the driver's seat with another blast of cold.

"If you're bringing Greta to the rec center today, let

one of us drive you," he growled, after swiping some of the moisture off his dark hair. Growling seemed to be his natural speaking style, when he didn't make an effort to hide it.

"Okay," she said, as if he had the right to tell her what to do. She liked him, after all—was *pretending* to like him. Wasn't that what you did, when you liked a man? Except...

He nodded, satisfied, and started the car for the short drive to Greta's. But all of this felt so strange—being met at the station, being given rides—that she had to try talking, even if it wasn't about simple information. "Trace, what do *you* get?"

"From what?" He almost grunted the words, what with paying close attention to the traffic, and to the pedestrians dodging trains, through the wet windshield.

She concentrated, hoping her words wouldn't mark her as a complete idiot. "You walk me to the station," she tried finally, a block later, glad he hadn't rushed her. "You pick me up. You drive me to the rec center, albeit with Greta, so that may be an outlier...."

"Outlier?" he repeated, as if he didn't quite understand, but she didn't dare pause to define the term or she'd lose her nerve.

"I appreciate the convenience, but what do you get? Why...?"

In no time, they were pulling into the cracked concrete drive in front of Greta's house. Trace braked and killed the headlights, but he didn't turn the ignition fully off. The heater drew chill from her skin. The windshield

wipers kept up their percussive vamp. Raindrops splat-
tered across the roof and windshield. He turned to her
with an are-you-serious? expression.

"Where'd you grow up anyway—a convent?" Maybe
he somehow noticed her inner flinch, despite her effort
to keep her expression safely impassive. Some of the
sarcasm eased off his dark features. "I get to know
you're safe. I get to spend time with you, maybe get to
know you. Figure out why…you know…."

None of which seemed a satisfying exchange for the
effort he was putting out. She was just…Sibyl. And, to
be technical, she wasn't even that.

He leaned closer—easy to do in a '70s-model sedan
with a bench seat. With a simple click of his seat belt,
Trace loomed over her quite thoroughly. "Why this," he
offered, his voice rough. Then he covered her lips with
a scratchy, damp kiss that set her head spinning into a
confusion of theses and speculations and corollaries and
oh…

The scent of him filled her nose, the taste of him
her mouth. He was so warm and wet and *there,* more
there than she could remember anyone ever being. She
fumbled handfuls of damp canvas off his shoulders to
hold on, as if otherwise she'd somehow fall through the
seat or the passenger-side door holding her up, fall right
out into the rain. She imagined that his shoulders were
broad enough, strong enough to hold on to through any
storm. Too soon, he drew back to nibble at her lower
lip, then to pull back from the kiss entirely. His eyes
searched hers, but she wasn't sure for what.

"That part doesn't suck either," he admitted, his voice rough.

She shook her head in agreement. No, it didn't suck. She wanted to say something witty about men being after Just One Thing, or how she might want a lot more chauffeuring at those rates, but speech didn't come easily even when she concentrated. With the distraction of him, right here...

"—back in a little over an hour," called a faint voice, past the rain. Trace's gaze lifted from Sibyl to the house. Sibyl twisted around to see, only realizing as his fingers drew off her that at some point he'd captured her waist. Greta Kaiser, complete with oversize umbrella, made her careful way down the house's front steps and toward the waiting car.

Trace cursed, kissed Sibyl quickly on the forehead and got out of the driver's side to go help. After blinking in the sudden silence—silence except for the rain and heater and wipers—Sibyl clambered over the seatback, so that Greta could ride shotgun. The temporary distance gave her a much-needed sanity break. This was *not* the way pretending was supposed to work!

And yet the longer the day lasted—Trace dropping her and Greta off, then picking them up again. Mitch sharing a delicious stew dinner afterward with them. All of them watching an old video together, with Sibyl comfortably tucked between Trace and the sofa's arm, marveling at the simple warmth and comfort of his nearness. The more time she spent with him, the more time she spent *in contact* with him, the harder it got to remember. She didn't really like Trace Beaudry-

LaSalle. She *couldn't* like Trace Beaudry-LaSalle. To do so would betray her father's memory, would betray the little, lost Isabel Daine that she'd once been.

She'd survived, as Sibyl, for one purpose only—a purpose that liking Trace could only complicate. To learn the truth—and to expose the whole damned society with it. See: *vengeance.*

So why didn't she feel more relieved when Trace took a call on his cell phone, and immediately looked guilty as he rolled to his feet and headed out for the hall? "Greta, you got a pen?" he called.

"In the kitchen, dear," Greta responded, preparing to stand.

Sibyl stopped her and went herself, getting the pen from the countertop container. When she handed it to Trace, he wouldn't quite meet her gaze.

"1217 East Pacific," he murmured, clearly repeating the caller's information as he wrote the address on his arm. "Tomorrow. 10:00 p.m. Got it." Silence. "Yeah. 'Course."

Then he disconnected—and looked at her. He seemed unhappy.

Sibyl cocked her head. She feared that if she asked him what was going on, he couldn't miss her nefarious motives. He would immediately realize that she was trying to get close to him only to uncover information about his relationship with his birth father. He wouldn't want to spend time with her anymore.

"Got a job," he admitted, returning the pen. "It's nothing."

She nodded, even as she thought: *If it's nothing, why are you looking so guilty?*

And what kind of a job starts so late at night?

And why don't I feel validated, to have this kind of lead?

Climbing back onto the sofa beside him, curling into the space under his arm and against his ribs, she didn't have as hard a time differentiating the fantasy of liking him from the reality of spying on him.

But spying on him felt nowhere near as satisfying.

The very next time she saw Trace Beaudry, he'd unleashed his inner beast—and was pummeling another man into a bloody pulp.

Chapter 5

Everyone has their natural talents.

Trace Beaudry's was beating the crap out of people. People who asked for it, anyway. He'd grown up big for his age, the kid that other boys targeted to prove their toughness. Having no dad in the picture hadn't helped.

Learning to fight sure had.

Even his freshman year of high school, before Judge LaSalle had pulled up outside his ma's double-wide in his fine town car to change their lives, Trace had done well on the school wrestling team. When most of the athletics at his new, college prep school turned out to be posh, stuck-up crap like golf and dressage and sculling, Trace had found a home with wrestling, boxing and martial arts. Maybe he hadn't had the education or the temperament for LaSalle's upper-crust world. Hell, he'd felt like an oversize, brain-damaged hick most of the time until Smith, Mitch and Quinn befriended him—and sometimes even after that. But he could always channel his frustrations into good, honest violence.

Nothing but his body and endurance and willpower versus another man's body and endurance and willpower. Simple as that.

And, in the case of illegal, NHB fighting? Nowadays he could make a hefty wad of cash, too. That's because no-holds-barred fights were being driven deeper and deeper underground, until even the states that allowed them—like Texas—ended up enforcing more and more rules, barring holds beyond the original three taboos of groin strikes, bites and eye-gouging. That made them holds-barred fights, and nowhere near as fun for the cheering, hooting crowds. People came to NHB fights for "the damage."

Whether on the giving or receiving end, so did fighters like Trace.

His first opponent in the warehouse that night was a Latino named Emilio, smaller than him in weight and height. That could have made Trace feel like a big bully, except that Emilio was a freakin' kickboxer, and a damned fast one at that. Trace had once seen a kickboxer take down a sumo wrestler in a matter of seconds. None of his size or strength was worth squat if he couldn't get close enough to the guy to grab him.

The crowd cheered and hooted, but the fighters only saw each other. They circled the fenced, octagonal cage, Emilio flying at Trace feetfirst, Trace doing his damnedest to catch one of the guy's feet in midair.

So far, Emilio had kicked him in the ribs, grazed his freakin' forehead and slammed into his thigh—a few inches lower, and Trace wouldn't have a working knee. Trace had caught one of Emilio's kicks, but not good enough to hold on. When he compromised by throwing the guy, his opponent rolled out of the way before Trace could pin him against the chain link. Barefooted, bareknuckled—bare everything except for what their shorts covered—the two men circled. Emilio favored his left shoulder, where Trace had thrown him. Trace favored his right leg. Both grinned at each other like bloodthirsty animals, glad for the chance to see just what they were made of.

For the weirdest moment, Trace had a non-memory of doing the same thing with large, valuable swords. *Somewhere in the countryside, weighted by leather armor and heavy helmets...*

He snapped back fast enough when Emilio came at him with another flurry of murderous kicks. Instead of dancing back again, Trace dodged around them and tackled his opponent, hard, to the floor. A quick tightening of his hold, and yeah—the kickboxer, deadly legs trapped beneath their combined weight, was his.

"Submit!" Trace snarled, and started walloping the guy. Hell, it was disrespectful, not just to the crowd but to his opponent and to himself, to do anything but beat the crap out of him. Emilio could stop it anytime. He could tap out. Everyone tapped out eventually.

Emilio curled protectively into himself, snarling back something in Spanish.

Trace hit him again, a kidney shot. Nothing but a

grunt. Again. Both their bodies lurched at the force of the blows. The crowd seemed frenzied. Emilio just laughed through his own pain, so Trace hit him again—

Which is when he heard it. A single cry.

Somehow, through the cheering and the booing. Through the smoke and cell phone rings. Through his and Emilio's grunts and gasping breaths. Through his own rushing blood and pounding heart.

Somehow, Trace knew that voice.

Sibyl?

That's all it took, that momentary break in concentration. Somehow Emilio got an arm loose and, worse, hooked it around Trace's neck and began squeezing. Now Trace began to hit him faster, trying to break his hold, but his opponent stayed dogged. Trace's blows began to loose power, and…

Sibyl?

With a body-shaking thud, he fell to his side on the dirty warehouse floor, and for a moment he thought he saw her face, small and pale and Faline-eyed in horror, amidst the wild crowd. He didn't want that. He didn't want her to see him like this.

Then everything went black.

Not everyone tapped out, after all.

"Are you certain you wish to get out here?" demanded the cabdriver in his thick, Middle Eastern accent.

Sibyl counted out the correct number of bills, plus a tip. "Yes."

"I would not wish to get out here," insisted the cabbie.

And yes. With the exception of a surprising number of cars and pickups parked at the side of the road and in a vacant lot, the old warehouse district beside the Fairpark neighborhood felt dingy and deserted.

And dark, thought Sibyl, amusing herself with alliteration. And dangerous. "I wish to."

"I cannot wait for you here," he told her as she paid, and even looked sorry for that.

"No," agreed Sibyl, getting out. "Thank you."

Then the cab drove away, and she stood alone, her senses on alert. Otherwise, she wasn't particularly frightened. Growing up in a hellhole tended to readjust one's sense of real threat. People who actively trolled the streets, looking for prey, would find better hunting grounds than this. No, these men would have come for other purposes.

Sibyl's spy-against-the-Comitatus side saw infinite possibilities here, most of them scandalous. Was Trace dealing drugs? Moving stolen property? Could LaSalle be involved?

Disreputable. Dishonest.

In contrast, the confused-by-her-feelings Sibyl wanted this to be a mistake. Because Trace wasn't dishonest, no matter how much LaSalle blood flowed through his veins. No matter how guilty he'd looked on making this mysterious assignation. At least…she didn't want him to be dishonest. But if wishing could change things, her father would still be alive. She would never have accepted the scholarship to the New Orleans academy. She would have grown up like a normal girl.

She shook her head. "Not physics. Reality doesn't

change based on presence or wishes of observer." Her old, once-soothing habit of talking to herself, even in a whisper, wasn't a good sign. She had to get this over with. Like with Schrödinger's cat, she wouldn't know how to proceed until she looked in the metaphorical box.

"1217 East Pacific," she reminded herself—she needn't write things like that down. She inhaled deeply to settle her nerves, not that she could smell anything beyond city—asphalt, car exhaust, garbage—on the brisk air. She thought she heard something, many voices, shouting. But it faded almost as soon as she placed the thought, and could easily have been the wind itself, rushing through the smattering of distant trees. And...

There! Someone with lesser instincts might dismiss the sudden, peripheral impression of movement as imagination. Sibyl had lived too long only one mistake away from hurt and humiliation. She headed where she'd sensed the change.

She gave wide berth around the corner of a hulking warehouse, to minimize chances of an ambush, and so got a good view of several men loitering with feigned nonchalance at several points outside a freight doorway. A lookout, she thought of the one nearest her. And of the farthest, nearer the distant railroad tracks? Another lookout.

The third, she couldn't label so easily.

They certainly saw her. But she clearly didn't concern them, either in a good or bad way. So she headed closer, one step at a time.

Ah, now she definitely heard strains of a shouting crowd. No real music—not a rave, despite the undertones of illegality. She wished it *were* a rave, and Trace working as a bouncer or bodyguard, there to help anyone foolish enough to get into trouble with drugs or fights or underage drinking. But no. Muffled cheering. Faint booing. Like…a sporting event. Obviously, to judge from the area, hour and lookouts, a *criminal* sporting event.

Cockfighting? Sibyl felt increasingly sick from the narrowing possibilities. Dog fighting? She thought of Greta's happy, wiggly cocker spaniel, and her stomach clenched. Animals like little Dido were often used as bait to train the real fighting dogs. Despite the futility of wishing, she wished anyway. Please, no, Trace. Please, no.

The man directly in front of the sliding freight door—not unlike the door on her borrowed condo—stepped into her path.

They studied each other.

He stood bigger, wider than Trace, his dark skin and clothes helping him blend into the shadows. The style of his facial hair—thick here, thin there—made no sense to her. One of his jacket pockets sagged, with a gun probably.

And here she stood, small, insubstantial, unarmed except for the pepper spray in her own pocket. But she refused to lower her gaze. No weakness.

He grinned, a white semicircle of teeth against his bad-guy pose. "Twenty dollars."

Now she got it. Ticket taker.

"Ladies drink free," Sibyl challenged him, and he laughed.

"Good point, babe, good point. Go in and draw more business for us, yeah?"

She neither nodded nor declined, just waited for him to pull open the door.

Noise swamped her as she stepped inside. So did the sudden warmth generated by so many crowded bodies, and smoke from cigarettes and from less legal substances. She could smell beer and liquor and human sweat. But the noise felt like a physical assault. She wove her way through the crowd, knowing that to stand still would make her appear confused, weak. She ignored the entrepreneurs hawking dirty coolers full of bottled refreshments, and the apparent pimp, two girls not much older than her under each of his arms. She wished she could ignore the people laying bets, either with money or ego. "My money's on the big one," shouted one chunky, redneck type and she ducked by, and his skinnier friend said, "I dunno, that Messican looks awful fast."

Now she could see chain fencing, easily eight feet high, apparently the ring where this match took place. As she approached it, she thought she could smell blood. *Trace, no.*

But, no matter how loud the shouts, she should hear some kind of animal noise, shouldn't she? Perhaps dogs fought silently, without barks, but wouldn't they at least snarl? Yelp? All she heard was an occasional "oof!"

Like—a *human* oof.

Finally, she cut far enough through the press of the crowd to see the truth. Not cockfighting. Not dog fighting. Just…fighting. Two large men wearing shorts and nothing else grappled with each other, sheer strength against sheer strength—and the larger was Trace. Her Trace.

Her…?

Now that she recognized him, Sibyl couldn't tear her eyes from his swarthy, sweaty near-nakedness. Broad shoulders. Tree-like limbs. Pure, physical power. His muscles gleamed and bulged. He and his opponent bared their teeth at each other, like wild animals, as they circled. The reek of violence filled the warehouse like the cheers of the maddened crowd, especially when the smaller man flew at Trace, feet first. Trace somehow dodged the kick. With a bull-like lunge, he tackled his opponent, hard, to the floor. Using his strength, his size, his power, Trace began to punch him. Again. Again.

Their bodies lurched with each blow. Violent. Raw.

Sibyl's stomach twisted. So why couldn't she look away? Where did the sudden, primal thought of *I'm with him* come from?

She should be willing the other man to yell for help, as if they were in an alleyway instead of a fenced ring. To bargain. To do anything. Not just get…beaten. She forced herself to disassociate from Trace and imagine herself as his victim. At another, particularly brutal blow, a more familiar cry cut through the chaos around Sibyl.

Her cry.

Trace's head turned a mere fraction from his assault— and his full attention smashed into her. His eyes widened. And in that split-second during which their gazes met,

Sibyl saw something she'd never expected to see in a true descendent of the Comitatus.

Shame.

That shame struck her all the harder for her recognition of it.

Her ownership.

What do I have to feel ashamed for? she wondered—but another moment bludgeoned its way past. In that moment, maybe less, Trace's seemingly helpless victim twisted. Struck. Wrapped him in arms and legs both, and held on.

Suddenly, Sibyl's concern lay less with Trace's opponent and more with her big, confusing lug. His piston-like blows began to lose power, faded into fumbling. Could he even breathe?

As he lurched toward the ground, seemingly lifeless, Sibyl's life seemed to sink with him.

For once, she didn't analyze.

She just ran, pushing and elbowing anyone in her path, practically climbing her way around the fenced enclosure to find her way in to Trace as he collapsed. The crowd erupted into cheering, into booing. Sibyl ignored them.

Sense or not. Violence or not. He mattered more.

Trace had a vague awareness of light and blurry faces. He barely remembered standing. Congratulating the winner. Staggering out of the octagonal ring without the money he'd come for. And then—

Sibyl.

Was she real, or not? As his head cleared, he found

himself sitting on a bench, out of the worst of the crowd. Someone even handed him an ice pack for his knee. But as the crowd's attention turned to the next fight, Sibyl reappeared. Instead of freaking out on him—crying, or scolding, or cringing away—she handed him a bottle of cold water. "Drink," she said firmly.

He drank. Then he faced the situation. "How'd you find me?"

"You said the address out loud, on the telephone. I was..." Her eyes darted away from him. "Curious."

"Yeah, well you're not safe here." The very idea of her traveling alone, to this neighborhood, washed his lingering disorientation away as thoroughly as the cold water.

Sibyl looked at the ice pack on his knee and raised her eyebrows. Little she might be, but something about her didn't seem anywhere near as young and helpless as before.

"Well I know what I'm getting into. But you shouldn't..." He scowled, then tried again. "I didn't want—why'd you have to come?"

She cocked her head. "You don't want me here?"

"What do you think?" He regretted his fierce response the moment it grunted out of him, but she didn't even flinch. How'd someone as tiny as her get this tough? "I didn't want you or the others to see me doing this."

"You're ashamed." She didn't make that a question.

"Hell, no!" That fast, he knew he wasn't. But then he had to figure out why he played the fights so close to his vest, around his highborn buddies. "These are good fights! And it's good money, because I kick butt at it, when I'm not distracted by little, nosy…distractions."

Her lips twitched into a smile, and he couldn't tell if she was laughing at him or with him, but as long as his words kept coming, he let them.

"Look, people think I should be ashamed, and that's bad enough, okay? They think extreme fighting is, you know…barbaric. Or 'vulgar.' And I don't want to try explaining why it isn't, when people like you already have your minds made up."

"My mind's not made up." And she was there—which was enough to give him nightmares all by itself. How had she…?

"You hate violence." He remembered something cute. "You hid your face in my shoulder during that movie at Greta's, when the bad guy got—"

"My mind's not made up," Sibyl insisted more loudly. Then she added, "There are no people like me."

That, he might agree with.

"Tell me." Sibyl sank gracefully onto the bench beside him as if he weren't sweaty and bloody and probably stinking. "Why isn't it vulgar?"

"It's real, is what it is. Honest fighting, not some cleaned up pretense of it, you know? Those college prep guys…they learn sword fighting with a bunch of rules, warm up first, wear the proper gear, three-minute bouts, fifteen touches and you're out." He hadn't sucked at fencing, especially with the heavier épée, but the rules had about driven him crazy. "Like in a real fight you'd never get 'touchés.' Like swords weren't invented to attack or defend at any cost. Like that Charlemagne guy would've given anyone fifteen 'touchés.'"

Sibyl looked down—he remembered that she didn't wholly like the swords.

"Or boxing," he continued quickly, wondering if he'd suffered a head injury, to be talking like this. Or maybe he just hoped she'd stay here, all clean and good-smelling, at least until he finished talking. "Rich folks go to boxing matches all the time. The senator who's been getting extreme fighting banned all over loves boxing. It's like if you toss in some stupid Marquess of Queensbury rules, that makes it okay. That hides the fact that it's still about one guy trying to pound the other into submission. It's a lie. In No-Holds-Barred fighting—at least we're honest."

She still hadn't fled him in disgust.

"It's not like we don't have any rules. You can't gouge eyes or hit a guy in his—or look at the bare knuckles." If she noticed his sudden edit, she didn't show it. "You think boxing gloves protect the other guy's skull, but they protect the fighter's knuckles. Boxers die of head injuries every freakin' year, but not NHB fighters. We can't do multiple head-strikes without breaking our hands. The hurricane fencing's safer for fighters, too, because falling against the ropes can give you a kind of whiplash, but the chain takes a guy's weight evenly. We almost always walk out of the ring on our own. Even if we are kinda bleary," he added, since he really couldn't remember whether she was there as he left the cage or not. "And…"

Should he say it? Ah hell. He was being honest so far.

"And Sib, I'm good at it. When I fight, I'm me. For a few years there, I kind of lost track of that. I was trying to be who my dad wanted, and then to be whatever my dad didn't want, and it got me all twisted up. But the confusion goes away when I fight. Maybe that's why I like that sword so much. Because it connects me to other fighters in my family, and not just...not just the bad guys."

And there it was. More truth than maybe he'd ever realized on his own. Definitely more than he'd ever told a woman.

Sibyl watched him as she took it in. He liked that she didn't seem to make snap decisions, that she really seemed to see *him,* to hear *him,* in all his sweaty, oversize, whatever-the-opposite-of-glory was.

Then she smiled the smile that had first hit him in the gut with the thought *Mine.* It worked exactly the same way this time.

"Can you fight again tonight?" she asked. "Or did I get you disqualified?"

He hadn't scared her. He hadn't disgusted her. She looked at him, and she saw *him*—and she was smiling at him?

He grinned right back at her. "No guts, no glory."

Chapter 6

He won. Whether the presence of his "fair lady" had anything to do with it, Trace couldn't tell, but that one win earned him more than a month of day labor would have. He handed the stash to Sibyl, to hide in her cowboy boots, as he stiffly pulled on his clothing. He was going to hurt like hell, once he came down off the adrenaline. But pain was honest, too.

He followed her as close as a bodyguard as they made their way out through the crowd, putting the fear of God into anyone who looked too closely at her or her cute butt. Sibyl seemed surprisingly comfortable with them.

"I thought you didn't like people," he challenged, once they reached the relative silence of the morning-dark warehouse district.

"Not all people. Just powerful puppet masters

who hide their evil behind anonymity and don't care who they destroy to get their own way." Uh-huh. She shrugged her slim shoulders. "The guys back there are just lowlifes."

"Lowlifes can be dangerous." His limp was proof of that. Damned knee.

"I can handle them." Yeah, sure. "At least I can see them coming."

As opposed to the Comitatus? But he was too damned tired for more conversation. He even let her drive the car Mitch had loaned him, as long as she agreed to dig some money out of her boot for a twenty-four-hour drive-through.

"Your wish is my command," Sibyl promised him, starting the car.

Trace kept his eyes closed, both to rest and to avoid cluing her in on any further wishes he might have…not that he could follow through on any of them tonight, even if she were willing. But it didn't hurt to wish.

Especially since his attraction toward her had somehow shifted beyond merely finding her cute to finding her…special. Accepting. Honest.

Okay, so the pain *kind of* sucked.

By the time Sibyl pulled the car to a shuddering stop in the driveway of Greta's old Oak Cliff house, Trace had fallen asleep. So much for impressing him with her mad driving skills. She cut the engine, then spent a few minutes just considering him in the wash of a street-light.

The way she softened inside fascinated her, and not

just because of how long she'd kept a distrustful distance from most people. More from the sticky, dizzying effect he'd had on her earlier, as she'd watched him wipe down all that sweaty, tanned, dark-haired muscle after the second fight, his broad, naked chest, his bulging arms, his impossibly thick, planed legs…

"Lust," she defined to herself, as quietly as possible— that she was talking to herself again showed how unsettled she felt. "Not love. Lust. Normal."

Except she wasn't normal. After what the Comitatus had done to her…*no!* She mustn't lose herself in the memories again. *Look at Trace. Trace is safety.*

He really, really was. She'd seen how powerful he could be. To be on his side…*but you're not. He's Comitatus.*

But *was* he?

Trace Beaudry wasn't polished-handsome, not like the wealthy boys she'd known at school—points in his favor right there. He wore his hair short for fights, but only shaved now and then. His nose showed more than one break. Tonight's shadows gave his features a faint hint of caveman, big and hard and capable of terrible violence…

But not toward her.

He wouldn't hurt her. She knew that, beyond all doubt, because he'd risked his life for her. Because he'd had numerous opportunities to overpower her, and hadn't. What he'd said…well, she knew better than to believe mere words, because people lied, even to themselves. But what people did, that was truth.

He's Comitatus. But the reminder carried less and

less power the more often she tried using it to distance herself from her feelings.

He looked so gentle now, his eyes closed like that, his mouth slack. She remembered what his lips would feel like under hers, and shifted in her seat, bit her lower lip.

No guts, no glory.

Sibyl leaned across the parking brake and breathed in the scent of him—sweat and blood, yes, and fast-food onion and sweet chocolate from a shake, but so very real. Real enough to keep all manner of boogeyman, real and imagined, far away.

Dipping her head even closer, Sibyl pressed her lips to his scraggly cheek and kissed him.

Real warmth. Real scent. Real whiskers against her lips.

Real man.

She drew back, eyes wide, and tasted salt. She watched him wrinkle his nose, and clear his throat, and open his eyes—which slanted to her side of the car.

She stared and said nothing, her heart racing and her mind…not.

He frowned as if confused, then blinked the expression away and grinned sleepily at her. "Hey. You got us here in one piece, huh?"

She nodded.

"Hope I didn't snore." At that, he hauled himself—with a louder, pained groan at his injuries—out of the car. He *had* snored, just a little. See: *once-broken nose.* But Sibyl hadn't minded. *Real.*

"You're staying here tonight." He made it like an

order, so she immediately considered arguing. But the light-rails had stopped running hours ago. She would have to borrow Mitch's car or call a cab to get back to the West End, where she didn't want to be anyway, and she didn't have the money to hire—

Oh. Actually, she had over a thousand dollars in her boots. Was Trace that tired, or did he really trust her that much?

She scrambled after him, kind of wishing he didn't trust her like this.

God knew she'd stopped being trustworthy a lifetime ago. When he insisted on her taking his bed, promising to sleep on the sofa, and staggered off to the shower across the hall, Sibyl used that opportunity to look through the drawers of the one antique dresser in his room, deliberately avoiding the medieval short sword laying dramatically on top of it. Sure, she didn't find anything more damning than a pack of condoms, nor more useful than an old white T-shirt to sleep in—which hung on her like a tent until she knotted part of it at her waist. Sure, she finished by tucking his winnings under his socks. But that didn't ameliorate the fact that she was still spying on him—the guy who valued honesty so much. That didn't mean that, had she found something to use against his father or the Comitatus, she wouldn't have leapt on it, even if she'd had to steal Mitch's car to secret her find away.

Her relief didn't make her any more trustworthy, anymore than Marquess of Queensbury rules made boxing less dangerous than NHB fighting.

Crawling into Trace's bed, surrounded by the smell

of him, Sibyl couldn't possibly sleep. She listened to the shower across the hall. She imagined Trace in there, washing all that blood and sweat off his warrior's body. Why hadn't it bothered her more?

Because it's his.

The horror she'd felt when she'd thought him hurt or dead, the odd ache in her chest when he'd all but dared her to be disgusted by him. She didn't need experience she didn't have, or the IQ she did, to face what this had become. She only needed a little courage.

She was falling in love with Trace Beaudry. Trace Beaudry-LaSalle…no. That just confused things too much. Just let him be Trace.

Despite her best efforts. Despite excellent reasons not to. Despite the fact that it couldn't possibly end well—not that anything did, for her. The lie had become truth. She was falling in love with Trace.

The weight of keeping that from herself eased off her slim shoulders. The futility of fighting it brought its own kind of relief, of stillness. Sibyl snuggled deeper into his bed, breathed his safe, male scent off his pillows and imagined him in the shower, naked, with curiosity instead of fear—

Then she jolted awake, sitting straight up at the sight of him filling the doorway.

The door must have woken her.

As her eyes adjusted to the faint hall light framing him against the dark room, she saw that he wore nothing but a towel, slung low on his hips. And…oh! Even with most of him in shadows, Trace was stunning. Broad shoulders eased into an equally broad chest, masculine and hairy. The chest—and the hair—tapered down his abs into narrow hips....

And then the towel. Stupid towel.

Sibyl would have had to lean forward to pick up this line past his equally furry, tree-trunk thighs to check out his knees and calves, but she couldn't move.

"Sorry," rasped Trace. "Forgot—need clothes for downstairs."

Better than forgetting she was in his bed, she guessed. She watched him shuffle to his dresser, stiff and sore. Practically dead on his feet. And she thought she was tired?

How bad a beating had he taken tonight, anyway? In the shadows, she had little hope of making out his bruises. But he gave her his bed and planned to take the stairs down to the sofa, anyway.

Chivalry—the real kind, the honorable kind—wasn't dead.

"Stay here," she said quickly, before she could chicken out.

Trace paused mid-shuffle and looked dumbly at her. Then he shook his head. "You get the bed."

Idiot. But she wouldn't say that, wasn't sure she wholly believed it. Instead, she threw back the covers, showing some leg. "With me. Stay here."

His brow furrowed as he seemed to search for reasons he knew he should object. But sleepy people were easily led, one reason sleep-deprivation made such a good torture technique. Like the kind Comitatus conquerors were once so fond of.

Shut up.

"Now," Sibyl insisted firmly. To her surprise, with a shrug of defeat, Trace turned and sank stiffly onto the bed. She grasped a handful of fitted sheet to keep from rolling into him as the mattress tipped. "Good. Now lie down."

He obeyed, though with a less-than-docile snort. "If you're thinking to molest me, you're gonna have to do all the work. Not that I'm not...you know..."

She smiled at him, an unfamiliar warmth spreading through her, and offered the appropriate quote. "'The spirit is willing but the flesh is weak'?"

"Yeah." He yawned. "That. 'Cept, not *weak*."

"Spent?" she suggested, stretching the covers back over them both and snuggling back down. Now the bed *really* smelled like him. Damp, and clean, and warm, and *here*. And she was falling in love. As much as she was capable which, luckily, probably wasn't much.

"No promises about tomorrow, either." Even as she wondered whether that meant yes or no to having her wicked way with him, he added, "But if you aren't, you know, serious? Go downstairs now." He yawned again. "Or wake up first."

"You're not a saint," she agreed happily, wiggling closer to his curved, bitable shoulder. "Not even like William of Gellone."

Even now, she hoped that sword of his came from one of the other French heroes, and not Charlemagne. Not the conqueror.

"Damned right..." But the last of his sentence faded away, followed by a slow, deep breath.

Listening to his breathing—even more soothing than

the shower—she tentatively slid a hand over his upper arm, then onto the arch of his chest. She'd been right. Furry. She spread her fingers into the surprising softness and warmth.

His breathing stuttered, then continued.

She slid one slim leg over his, her knee grazing his damp towel. He probably shouldn't sleep in that. She had no idea how to get it off him without waking him again. Oh, well.

Tucking her nose and forehead against his upper arm, Sibyl relaxed back into sleep.

With Trace.

Trace woke suddenly, tense and alert. What…?

He tried to sit up, but at least seven different parts of his body screamed at him not to move, so he lay still again. The sun hadn't risen yet. So what had disturbed him?

Uh-oh.

Someone lay in bed with him. Someone soft, and small and female. Someone who smelled like books, and autumn, and—oh.

He relaxed, remembering. Not some nameless one-night stand. *Sibyl.*

Then his battered body started to revive at the thought. *Sibyl?*

And what had woken him?

Then he heard it again, and recognized it from his slowly waking memory.

A whimper.

"No," she whispered, curling farther into herself.

Since she was hugging his arm like a teddy bear, and had a naked leg on top of his, she couldn't achieve full fetal position. *"No."*

That had to be one hell of a nightmare. "Hey," he whispered, his voice hoarse from last night's near strangling. "Hey, Sib."

She bolted upright, eyes wide. "What?"

"Shhh. Don't wake Greta."

She stiffened, maybe as surprised to wake with him as he was with her. He could see her in the gray pre-dawn, her long hair mussed, a tent-size T-shirt—his?—dangerously close to sliding off her shoulder. To his relief, she lay back down and wove her arms around his upper arm again. "Sorry."

"'S'all right."

She tried to slide her smooth, bare leg over his again—and her bare knee brushed evidence of just how all right he was. "Oh."

Damn. How long had it been since he'd woken at full flag?

"Sorry," he muttered, forcing a few stiff muscles to move enough to study her startled face. Musta lost the towel. *Virgin,* he reminded himself grimly. No way could he ask her to take the reins on this one—assuming she was even interested—and he really wasn't in any shape to act on this himself. He wasn't sure he could even drag himself to the bathroom to take care of things solo—and he sure as hell wasn't going to tend to himself with her right beside him.

To his relief, she looked startled but not disgusted.

In fact, she bit her lower lip, then shyly asked, "May I touch?"

He doubted this could end well, but even he didn't have the strength to hold back the "Hell, yeah," that leapt out of him. "I'm naked and in bed with you. Permission's kind of…"

"Implied?" But he didn't agree with her because she'd just slid her hand down his front, as if savoring the feel of him, until her fingers glided up his erection. "Oh!"

Don't come yet. Don't come yet. You're not fifteen. Think about, uh…

"You haven't even made it to third base?" he managed to grunt as her soft fingers explored the length and width of him.

"No," she whispered, and he heard a surprising smile in her words as she experimented with one finger, then with her whole hand.

"So, not even—" he grit his teeth at the heaven of her palm encircling him. She bit her lip again. Worried? Disgusted? No, to judge by the refreshing sparkle in her eyes, this anatomy lesson fascinated her. Now she began to slowly stroke him. *Oh,* crap. He was so gonna screw this up.

"Is this third base?"

"God, yes."

"Then no."

Somehow, he managed to capture her wrist, even as his baser instincts cursed the sudden nobility. "Look, Sib, I've got bruised ribs, a bad knee and God knows what else going on. You're on your way to making me feel ten kinds of wonderful, but I'm not in any shape to repay you tonight, so I'll probably just fall asleep afterward like some ass. You want better than that."

She sat up, despite his hold on her wrist. Her body pushed even more of the covers off them, and he caught a glimpse of her panties under the bunched edge of his shirt. How could someone he'd once considered merely cute have such shapely legs?

"I don't want better than that," she told him solemnly.

Way to make a guy feel special. He was going to tell her that she should—but then she simply said, "I want you."

At that, no amount of nobility or pain could have stopped him. Staring at her in amazement, he let go of her wrist. But instead of recapturing his erection with her hand, Sibyl cocked her head—then bent at the waist, her hair sweeping his abs like a curtain, and tasted him.

Trace nearly bucked off the bed, but he could barely tell the difference between hurt and heaven. He had one hell of a good clue.

Heaven came with Sibyl.

Sibyl had never felt so tightly drawn, so powerful. She explored Trace's amazing body with her hands, with her tongue, kissing and tasting and returning, again and again, to the most obvious proof of his masculinity. Her mind powered down and instinct took over. He moved under her and bit back groans, or moans—she couldn't quite tell the difference. Finally, he wrapped his hand around her head and held her there, so she guessed he must be getting impatient. So she practiced taking him deeply into her mouth, the way some girls bragged about. He almost didn't fit, no matter how wide she opened. So why wasn't she frightened of him penetrating her in even more intimate ways?

Because he won't hurt you.

Somehow, over the last days, she'd accepted that. Unclenching from her hair, he slid his hand down her cotton-covered back and into her panties, from behind. His callused palm cupping her butt felt amazing. When his fingers probed between her legs, she stiffened, lost track of the rhythm she'd begun to find—and he immediately retreated.

He won't hurt you. But was that necessarily a good thing? Would it rob her of the completion, the satisfaction, that her body needed with increasing vehemence?

Trace began to buck under her, his teeth gritted, his noises muffled and guttural. Before she knew what had happened, he'd grasped her clumsily with both hands, one on an elbow, one behind her back, and dragged her bodily upward while he arched off the bed, biting back sounds that wanted to be shouts. She felt something warm—ejaculate, she supposed—splatter against her hip, but then he was kissing her between gasps, clearly more than pleased.

"I did it right?" she whispered. His laughter—and a few curses that somehow came out approvingly—joined the kisses and the gasps.

Now was when he would go to sleep like he'd warned her. She knew better than to mind, despite the way her foot kept dragging up and down his leg to feel the friction of his hair and the hardness of his muscles, despite the throbbing deep inside her that seemed to be begging for more, more. Not his fingers, not yet. Those had startled her. But...

"Take off your panties," Trace growled, apparently having forgotten his disabilities.

Sibyl's insides jumped at the command, half in excitement, half in concern. He'd warned her. She hadn't gone downstairs. So whatever happened now, she'd invited, right? No. Wrong. She could leave at any time—and he would let her. That knowledge stilled the worst of her fears.

Instead of digging a condom out of the stash she'd already found in his bed table, Trace—with a long groan—slid off the bed and onto the floor, where he knelt beside it. Beside her. "C'mere."

"You aren't asleep."

"Nope." When she didn't obey, he simply caught one of her legs and turned her easily on the bed. He caught the waistline of her panties with his thumbs, then paused to frown at her from below. "You okay with this?"

She tried to speak, but although her lips moved, no voice came out. She meant to shake her head. She wasn't ready, she was terrified. But somehow, it came out as an honest nod, instead.

With one smooth pull, Trace had dragged her panties down her legs and off her feet, then eased her knees apart. *Now? Already?* She felt the shock of cool November morning against her damp body...and then, even as she reeled from that, his hot breath replaced it as he bowed his head between her legs—and kissed her. *There.*

"Ohh…." She wasn't—she didn't—all she knew was that the sensations shuddering through her felt more than okay. Sibyl let her knees drift wider apart, amazed by the delicious rasp of Trace's whiskers against her inner thighs, against even more tender flesh. The gentle suction of his kiss, and then his tongue—"Ah!"

"I can sto—" he started to say, but she shifted her feet so that her knees straddled his shoulders, holding him against her. That's how much she trusted him. His chuckle, into the center of her body, tickled in better ways than she could ever have imagined. And when he really began to nuzzle against her, to truly suckle her…

That's when the real whimpers started.

She'd never…she'd tried to satisfy herself, of course, but that had only…oh! No wonder this was all some of the girls in juvie could talk about! Her full, physical awareness of him…the amazement that he would take this kind of trouble, just to make her feel…and he wasn't hurting her, just building, just encouraging…

She began to writhe, to thrash against him, until he reached upward with his hard, long arms and caught her under the arms with his broad hands. His thumbs kneaded her breasts through the cotton of the oversize T-shirt, his fingers held her down. She still bucked, but he kept her from shaking him off. His tongue felt so thick and hot and wonderfully invasive. His teeth brushed her in a flicker of danger. He was worshipping her in the most carnal ways she could imagine, and something was about to…it scared her, and she needed to hold on, but…she needed *it,* needed *him,* needed… needed…

"Trace!" Her heels dug into the flesh of his back as Sibyl all but launched herself off him and the world exploded. *She* exploded. She shattered into fragments of memories and pain and long lost hopes and stolen glories. The heavy walls of isolation around her crumbled. *She* fell apart completely, shuddered into nothingness, gasped for breath she could never catch without lungs, clawed for purchase she would never find without flesh.

And then he was back on the bed, on her, drawing her pieces back together with ease, kissing her with a mouth that tasted damp and warm and fascinatingly like…like her. He cuddled her against him, where she felt so safe. One of his big hands cupped her between the legs, and a finger swirled in the hot, needy damp there, and she said, "Yes, yes, yes," into his mouth, until the finger slid into her. It didn't hurt. She writhed happily against him, kissed him with more than she thought remained of her, so he tried a second finger, and that felt tight but still better, still necessary, and she wondered if this was what it would feel like if he just mounted her and thrust into her, which was when he tried three fingers—

She exploded again, even harder than before, but Trace's kisses muffled her ecstatic scream. And the one after that. And after that, too.

And then he'd freed his magical hand and rolled onto his back, grinning—until she began to weep into his arms. Then his face fell.

"I *hurt* you? God—"

"Shut up," she growled, and gave him salty kisses. He tentatively kissed her cheeks in return, kissed her clean of her tears, kissed her until her breath returned in slow, steady waves full of the smell and nearness of him.

"You're okay?" he rasped finally, gently.

She nodded, then tried to show him how okay she was by catching his mouth again. He met her, kiss for kiss, but sank back into the tangle that had been his bed as he did. His breath caught in a way she couldn't miss and, embarrassingly, recognized from earlier in their proceedings as well. Not just passion.

Bruised ribs. Hurt knee—and he'd been kneeling? He'd said he would sleep.

"You're going to regret this in the morning," she chided, somehow unable to move out of the solid, naked support of his arms, even so.

"Not hardly," he assured her. "Just dream good dreams this time, okay?"

She nodded. She would have nodded at almost anything. Dead father, or not. Years of vengeful planning, or not. Trace had moved past being a means to avenging her past and instead, for the first time, had her wondering about a completely different future.

She would do anything this man ever asked of her, and gladly. Because of an orgasm? Well, a handful of orgasms, but still. No, because of so much more. If that made her stupid, she'd be stupid.

Part of her feared a mistake—the kind of mistake that didn't just hurt her, but hurt innocent others. But at the moment, she wouldn't give that cynical, paranoid side any of her attention. Maybe never again.

For the moment, anyway, she had…

"Trace?" she whispered suddenly into the gray of early morning, as if she couldn't feel him under her, couldn't feel his arms surrounding her, couldn't smell his skin or hear his breath. She savored his name in her mouth.

"Yeah?" He sounded half-dead already.

I love you. But she didn't want to scare him. Didn't want to ruin this. Didn't want to act like the virgin that she still was. She still was a virgin, right?

But not for long, if she had anything to say about it. Not with him.

"Night," she whispered, and smiled at his answering grunt, and fell asleep.

Exhaustion warred against pain, breaking Trace's sleep into chapters. He woke with Sibyl on his chest, in his arms, each time until the last.

Then he woke alone, unsure if he'd dreamed the knock on the house door or her sudden scramble away from him. He pushed himself up onto his elbows and cursed out the pain through gritted teeth.

Alone.

With voices downstairs. Greta's. Sibyl's.

And some guy he didn't recognize.

Now he remembered Sibyl's concerned whisper of, "Greta!" He launched himself out of bed—or would have. If he hadn't just fought two bouts, one of them all three rounds, of no-holds-barred last night, then complicated matters with everything-but sex. Instead, he staggered. Straightening to his full height would take too long, so he stayed bent as he pulled on a pair of boxers. He almost fell, twice. But finally he managed to stagger into the hallway—taller with every step—and toward the narrow old stairs.

On the landing, however, he met Mitch, fully dressed in khakis and one of those Mexican shirts he favored, just standing there.

"Out of the way," Trace started to snarl. But he only managed "Oum?—" before Mitch pinched his mouth shut.

"Shh! He shouldn't know we're here."

Trace glared pure murder at the smaller, blonder man, and growled low in his throat. But he'd forgotten something about Mitchum Talbott.

The guy didn't actually scare.

Sure, he put on a great "gosh, golly" front, and pre-ferred talk to violence any old day. But when push came to shove, like Trace's idea of shoving his friend down the stairs in order to get to Sibyl? The guy stood his ground.

"Who?" he managed to mumble, through the side of his mouth.

Mitch, seeing that Trace was trying to keep his voice down, let go.

"Dillon Charles," he clarified. "From the Comitatus. Looking for you."

Chapter 7

Dillon freaking *Charles?* The first person to have soured Trace on the supposed nobility of the Comitatus? The pretentious jerk who'd worked from the start to corrupt what tiny chance Trace might have had at forging a relationship with his own father?

Trace made like a charging bull again.

Again, Mitch stepped directly into his path, finger to his own lips this time.

"—talk to the local…group…" Greta was saying, "I'm certain they will clarify matters for you."

Matters like her house being off-limits to anyone Comitatus. Matters like her having been granted sanctuary.

Charles asked, "And by *group*, you mean…?" He was trying to catch them in knowing more than they should, trying to learn who had broken Comitatus secrecy.

"You obviously know that better than we do," stated Sibyl in that solemn way of hers. "Why don't you tell us?"

Trace felt an unexpected surge of pride. *Way to go, Sibyl.*

"Not necessary," Charles assured her. "You say my… friend…isn't here, and I've clearly overstepped some sort of local…treaty." The word "treaty" did not come out sounding happy. "I'll go."

"That would be for the best," Greta agreed.

"By the way, what happened to you?" Mitch whispered, making a face at—oh. Trace had to look down at himself to remember just how brilliantly bruised he'd gotten. "Seriously. You look like you were in a tragic tie-dye accident."

"Yeah? Well, you look like someone I could crush with my—" Trace had to swallow back a howl of pain when Mitch grinned and poked one of his bruised ribs.

"Good day, Miss Kaiser," Dillon was saying to Greta. "Good day, Isabel." And Trace forgot about killing Mitch.

Who the hell was Isabel?

"There he goes," noted Mitch after a moment, cocking his head at absolutely nothing. Apparently he read Trace's confused expression. "The purr of a truly exquisite engine."

"It's safe now," called Sibyl.

In three strides, Trace reached the bottom of the stairs and pulled her tight against him, bruises be damned. She felt familiar and necessary and unexpectedly fragile.

Dillon freakin' Charles?

"He was here for your sword," she said softly, tipping her face up toward his, her cheek pillowed against his bare chest. "He knows you're here."

He shrugged. "So I'll leave."

She pressed harder against him. Ow. But it wasn't a bad hurt. What did she think he meant, leave Dallas? He only meant to leave Greta's!

"Whoa, Nelly." There Mitch went, talking again. "Before we make any big decisions about staying or leaving or plotting or not plotting, why don't we contact Smith, sit down as a group and weigh our options? You know…clothed? Not looking like you just slept togeth—oh, my merciful God, you two are *sleeping together?*"

And he thought Trace was the dumb one? Trace silently dared him to comment further, but for once Mitch said nothing. Good. Trace and Sibyl weren't open to discussion. Unless…

Trace glanced at Greta, unsure if he owed her an apology. This was her house, after all, for all that he paid rent on his room. God knew his Ma had never been one of those 'not under *my* roof you don't' types. But Greta was a lot older than Ma.

Greta showed no signs of disapproval. She seemed caught up in their unexpected visitor.

Sibyl, though, had stiffened away from his embrace. "I should go, then," she said, not looking at anyone—not even Trace. His T-shirt, hanging to her knees and flirting at the edge of one shoulder, made her look young and vulnerable. "Schmomitatus business."

"Wait," called Mitch, even as she put one tentative bare foot on a step to escape. "You're our answer girl. How does Dillon Charles even know you? I mean— Isabel?"

Isa…? Sibyl. Oh.

Trace couldn't help but stare. Dillon Charles knew her? Knew her well enough to know her real name?

Sibyl's eyes, lifting slowly to his, looked trapped. That, more than anything, stirred awake suspicions in Trace's gut.

Then she spun, deerlike, and fled up the stairs.

Sibyl had pulled on last night's clothes with shaking hands before Trace came in. Had he waited to give her privacy, or out of disgust?

He knew she'd been lying to him. She'd seen it in his eyes.

Just in time for it to matter to her. Just in time for everything else to go wrong, too. Dillon Charles had recognized her. And seeing him for the first time since the fire had ended her stay at his prestigious school— had ended her world—just sharpened all the pain that spending time with Trace had soothed.

"You can use the shower if you want," said Trace, upon arriving in his bedroom to see her already dressed. She couldn't blame him. She felt gross. Her clothes still smelled like beer and cigarette smoke from last night. Her skin still smelled like…

Him. That part, she didn't mind at all. But maybe he did.

She shook her head. "Have to go."

He scowled. "But Smith's on his way over."

Which just meant she had to go quickly. Smith's father currently headed the local Comitatus. She should trust him even less than the other exiles. So she shouldered her backpack purse. "Go…"

Her ability to speak hadn't failed her this badly since prison.

Trace reached a hand toward her, and she flinched. He could hurt her far worse than the others, even than Dillon Charles, whose lawyer father had helped send her to prison. Trace could hurt her for reasons far beyond his violent fighting abilities. And worse, she could hurt him.

He let his hand drop before touching her. Instead he asked, "Did I do something wrong?"

Hurt. Like that.

He stood there, swarthy and sturdy and bruised—God, she'd had no idea, last night, how many bruises—but unbent. Unshaven and nearly nude, he could have been a Neanderthal warrior, powerful enough to drag her to his cave, make her his—but also to kill any saber-toothed tigers that threatened her. He could be a knight of olde, momentarily stripped of his armor but no less dangerous. After all, chivalry only counted with the noblewomen. Peasant girls had been any lord's for the taking. Dillon Charles wouldn't have honored peasant girls.

Still, Trace had stripped his armor for her, this time.

And no. He'd done nothing wrong.

She shook her head. Then, because she had no sense

of self-preservation around him, she touched him, flattening her palms gently on his broad, bruised chest. She stood on tip-toe to lift her face, her mouth, hopelessly for his.

With a grunt of either pain or impatience, Trace caught her hips and lifted her to sit on his bureau. Then he enfolded her in his arms and completed the kiss.

She took another.

And another.

With hungry hands, she explored every undamaged bit of him that she could find. She wrapped her legs around his ribs, boots and all.

Her adrenaline-drenched blood thrummed through her with panicked rhythm—*have to go, have to go, have to go.* Everyone in this house, except for her and Dido the dog, came from Comitatus blood. The arrival of Smith, with or without his southern belle girlfriend, would only add to that. And Dillon Charles?

If she remembered correctly, he'd always gotten his way. He would be back.

He'd recognized her, after almost a decade since his father helped condemn her child self to prison.

And yet…*Trace.* With a hand cupping her butt, he pulled her against his hardness, reawakening hunger for the same kind of feast he'd given her last night. His other hand spanned the back of her head, stroking her hair, encouraging her hot, needy mouth against his.

At one point he let her go to push her cowboy-booted ankles downward, so she dug at his butt instead of his—oops—his injured ribs. But almost immediately he'd cradled her head again.

She wanted…she wanted…

Hell, between turning down the volume in her busy brain and jacking up the volume in her five senses, she'd become nothing *but* want.

Reaching back to brace herself harder against him, her hand touched cold metal. She barely noticed until, as he rasped growling kisses down her throat, she curled her fingers onto the metal, clutched at—

"Ow!"

Trace leaned back, barely, and blinked at her like a man fighting hypnosis. His hands stilled. His body froze against hers. "What?"

Equally confused, Sibyl looked down at her stinging hand. At the odd slash of red across it.

Trace recognized the blood before she did. "The sword! Hold still."

Immediately he was in his duffel bag, presumably for bandages and antibiotic cream. Parts of Sibyl wished he were still kissing her—especially the parts that felt cold and dissatisfied from his sudden departure. But part of her…

Her brain…

The part that had kept her alive so far….

She twisted on the bureau and looked at that damned, ancient sword which she'd accidentally grabbed. A Comitatus sword, perhaps the sword of Charlemagne. Swords existed for one reason—to hurt and threaten those weaker than their warriors. Especially those who couldn't afford swords themselves. Which wasn't right.

No matter how sexy those warriors proved to be,

violence and domination and brutality could never be right.

"Here, hold this." Trace lay a cotton pad over the line of blood on her fingers—no spurting wound, no near amputation, just enough to wake her from last night's trance. "That sucker's sharper than I thought."

Sibyl shook her head. Her words fled, yet again—all of them except for *no, no, no.*

She slid off the bureau, onto the floor. Her boots made satisfying thumps on the floor, despite her small size. Despite her insubstantiality.

"Wait, I gotta disinfect—"

She dodged Trace and hurried out the bedroom door, rattled down the stairs.

"Sibyl, what gives?" She could hear him behind her, chasing her. *Chasing her.*

She moved faster, past the sound of Mitch and Greta chatting in the kitchen, past an inquisitive Dido the dog, to the front door. She fumbled to turn the knob with her left hand.

Thump. Trace's hand, big and hard, braced the door shut over her head. "Hey!"

She spun, stared up at him, trapped by his half-naked body. He really wouldn't hurt her. She believed that with everything she had left of a heart. But him and his LaSalle blood and his kindness and his protection and—oh, God—and his talented mouth and fingers and sex!

He'd trapped her, all the same.

"You need me to clean and bandage that wound," he insisted, and she saw peripherally that he held a handful of first aid supplies. "Not acting crazy would help, too."

Crazy. She'd pretended to be crazy sometimes, to survive prison. Maybe it hadn't been pretending. Sibyl breathed in the scent of Trace, stared up at his swarthy, whiskered face and reached—not for his face, but for his wrist. The one bracing the door shut. At some point she must have dropped the gauze. The touch of his skin hurt her palm.

Somehow, Sibyl managed another word, after all. She turned away from him, more fully toward the door. She looked one more time over her shoulder. She forced the breath—oxygen, fuel— to say, "Please."

Somehow, she must have convinced him. He moved his hand.

She fumbled the door open, then ran.

Behind her, Trace stood in the doorway watching until Sibyl turned a corner, out of sight. He didn't mind the frigid air, despite still being shirtless. This was Texas, after all, not Alaska. He had more serious business to sort out—something almost anyone would insist was not his strong point.

Her name was Isabel? She and freakin' Dillon Charles knew each other? Had the everything-but sex somehow scared her off—and how was he going to get her back, if it had? Because something had happened between them, not just in his bed this morning but at the match last night, and over the week or so before that. Something powerful, and delicate and important. Something that needed protecting. He had to get her back—or at least make sure she was okay, before he left her alone.

Instead, he stood there on Greta's front porch, shirtless and strangely unfeeling of the cold, until Smith Donnell and his girlfriend, Arden, pulled up in front of the house. Smith got out of the passenger side—it was Arden's car—but still came around to open the door for the dark-haired sophisticate. Because that's the kind of ladylike, chivalrous treatment Arden expected, so that was the kind of treatment she got.

Not for the first time, Trace found himself wondering what kind of treatment Sibyl expected.

"Aren't you cold?" drawled Arden as they reached him, something about her poise not making him feel at all like a clumsy, lecherous bull in an antique china shop.

Smith didn't hold to the same level of etiquette. "God, Trace, you look like you were playing paint ball naked—and I can't tell if the purples or the browns won. Go put on some clothes so we can figure out what to do about this Charles situa—hey, is that blood?"

Trace looked down and saw the smear of drying, red-brown on his wrist. Sibyl's blood. Way too close to his hand for comfort. He might not be into symbolism, but damn.

Suddenly, for reasons he couldn't begin to catalog, Trace felt sicker than he'd ever felt after the worst gut-punch he'd ever taken.

Dillon Napoleon Charles did not pace the handsomely understated den of the Fort Worth Donnell mansion.

He came from a long, long line of kings and heroes, descending from Charlemagne. He had better presence than that.

But he would very much have liked to pace.

Isabel Daine knew about the Comitatus?

"Good morning, Mr. Charles," drawled Will Donnell, strolling into the den with equal presence. Dillon had known the man's son, Smith, in college. Father and son favored each other; ironic, considering that the father now held local command of the society his son had rejected. The elder Donnell even wore blue jeans for this face to face meeting, instead of the expected business casual.

"Sir," Dillon greeted, choosing strained respect over what a more vulgar man might: something more like *good for whom?* or perhaps even *are you bloody well joking?* "I found my own morning troubling. As you are the area overlord, it seemed only fitting I come to you first."

"Please, call me Will." Will gestured to a pair of leather wingback chairs by the window. "I would offer you a drink, but considering the hour, can I ring for coffee?"

"No, thank you." *I'd probably just choke on it. Or spit it at you.*

Sinking into the offered seat, Dillon reminded himself again that with nobility came obligations—literally. Too many Comitatus members had forgotten the rule of *noblesse oblige.*

"So how are things New Orleans way?" Will settled

easily into the chair across from Dillon's. "I was sorry to hear about your father the other year."

"Thank you. Time has helped, and Judge LaSalle…" *Has been like a second father to me.* But to try to explain to this near-stranger the bond of LaSalle losing his only son—his only legitimate son, at least—and Dillon losing his father would have made for embarrassing pathos. "He has proven himself a strong leader for the New Orleans powers. You have suffered a regrettable loss of your own, sir, in your predecessor, Donaldson Leigh."

Will nodded.

"I fear that the rumors do not put the Texas Comitatus in the best light," noted Dillon. *Murdered by one of his own men?* "If a subordinate was turning rogue, you of all men should know how to handle it."

Because Will Donnell's own son had turned rogue along with several compatriots, including the base-born Beaudry. Their crime? What used to be called *lèse majesté,* criminal insubordination. History taught that an organization as finely tuned as the powerful, multi-national Comitatus could not last without strong levels of hierarchy.

Hence Dillon's respectful deference to a man for whom, in his heart, he felt nothing but disgust. Trace Beaudry had been a lost cause from the start, because of his illegitimacy. But Smith Donnell and Mitch Talbott? They'd been born of blue blood, deserving of all the rights Dillon still held. Something must have spoiled them, tainted them, and parents seemed as likely to blame as anybody.

Will clearly saw the direction of Dillon's thoughts—

about his son, if not the disgust—but he showed it only through a twitch in his tanned cheek. "Thankfully, that insubordinate was dealt with."

"And yet cracks remain in the propriety of your... branch of the society." Time to get to his point. "I fear this is not only a courtesy call, although I owe you that much as well, being in your territory. In my pursuit of property stolen from Judge LaSalle, I have discovered a troubling breach of secrecy under your very nose. Women, Will. Women, who know about the Comitatus."

Will raised his eyebrows, a surprisingly mild reaction. Not a good sign. "If you refer to a certain Ms. Greta Kaiser, I have no reason to believe she knows about us, despite her late father's involvement in the society. It was because of his blood, not any intelligence on her part, that I agreed to give her home sanctuary status."

Dillon stared. A grandfather clock ticked ominously.

"The assurance of our loved ones' safety is, after all, one of the benefits of belonging to the society," Will reminded him. As if simply belonging—knowing you were one of the best and brightest and most important—wasn't the ultimate benefit.

"The women knew enough to send me to you."

"By name? Did they use any words such as 'secret society' or 'Comitatus'? I have no cause to believe that anybody has broken his vow of secrecy."

"I'm not saying anybody did." Anybody like Will's son? Smith Donnell, as an exile, should be dead to his father, the way Trace Beaudry was as dead to the judge as René LaSalle Jr. How many undeserving types was Will protecting? "But Ms. Kaiser had a girl with her, a former convict named Isabel Daine. I knew the girl long ago, before her arrest for arson and patricide. She's something of a genius and, I believe, holds a grudge against us. She could be uncovering our secrets with or without the help of the exiles."

At least now, Will looked surprised. "How could she hold a grudge against us if nobody disclosed information?"

"It might behoove you to find out. You are the leader around here, aren't you?" Damn. The man's calm was pushing Dillon to flat-out insubordination. "Sir."

"But therein lies the problem. While we appreciate your assistance, we are not wholly ignorant of the goings-on at Ms. Kaiser's residence. We have reason to believe that she's taken in certain…outcasts. We have no evidence that they mean to cause trouble—"

You aren't looking for evidence is more likely, thought Dillon.

"—and barring that, it would be beneath me, in my position of authority, to acknowledge their existence. If exiled Comitatus members were given the chance to address members of the inner circles they might become a nuisance, pleading their innocence, petitioning for reinstatement, etc. I could, of course, send a subordinate to conduct the interview but, as you noted, our local powers are currently recovering from a grave loss in our late leader. With Leigh's murder so fresh, I've yet to find someone with both the appropriate intelligence and the necessary objectivity to retain the equanimity our position dictates. In fact, I was considering bringing in a member from the outside to gather information for us."

"Someone like me."

Now Will Donnell sat back, gratifying relief on his tanned face. "You would do that for us?"

"As I said, I am investigating the theft of an important artifact from Judge René LaSalle, and I have reason to believe that the exiles know something about it. May I have your permission to conduct an interview on your territory regarding both that theft and the threat of persons such as Isabel Daine?"

"Conduct interviews, yes. But, I apologize for any insult, yet recent events dictate I clarify. You do not have permission to conduct violence."

If he'd had less dignity, Dillon might have rolled his eyes. "There is a time and place for everything, sir. The rules of our society are, to me, sacrosanct."

"Thank you. Then I look forward to your report." And the two men shook. Dillon supposed Donnell might be somehow playing him, but to what purpose? He had to believe that, bad seed of a son or not, Will Donnell also followed the dictates of the society.

No violence against those *of the blood,* even after exile, except as ritual—an official combat or an overlord-approved execution, when an individual became a danger to the whole. Smith Donnell, Mitch Talbott, even Greta Kaiser remained safe as long as they posed no threat.

A bastard like Trace Beaudry, though, or a no-blood like Isabel Daine?

Dillon Charles could do anything he wanted to them, with his nobility intact.

Yet another benefit to being the best and the brightest.

Chapter 8

Smith had a plan. He was bossy that way—he always had a plan. Sometimes Smith's plans even worked.

Trace wouldn't have put money on this one, not even at the point of no return, as he and his friends strolled into one of downtown Dallas' marble-floored, glass-windowed, chrome-trimmed lobbies, all but deserted on a Sunday morning.

All except for the security guard manning the granite-countered station facing the front doors.

"Donnell et al, here to see Dillon Charles," announced Smith, all hoity-toity, as if he were wearing a five-thousand-dollar suit instead of jeans and a T-shirt. Trace sometimes wondered if having been raised with money would have given him the same way of walking, of talking, of holding his head and clipping his words. Just as well he'd escaped that particular flaw. He didn't want anything more to do with the upper crust, damn it. So how did he keep ending up on jobs like this?

While the guard glanced over his papers—as if he had so many notes, on a weekend—Trace leaned closer to Smith and Mitch and whispered, "He's gonna double-cross us." He didn't mean the guard.

Smith managed to kick him, without a single ripple in the charming-as-hell, you-want-to-help-me smile he'd turned on Security Guard Guy.

"Not until he authenticates the sword," whispered Mitch back, patting his messenger bag. They'd taken pictures of Trace's sword from several angles, then printed out 8x10 copies.

Trace scowled, less than sold on this part of the plan, as well. But when Charles contacted Smith through Smith's dad—head of the local Comitatus—that's how this meeting had gone down. Charles wanted to see "whatever that was that Trace stole from the LaSalle bungalow." *Stole.* Which made Trace want to pound the guy into the ground almost as much as the fact that he hadn't heard from Sibyl for half a week, not since she'd bolted out of Greta's the morning after when Dillon Charles showed up. Charles wanted what Trace had, and Smith wanted information about it, so they were having a big meet about it, blue bloods to blue bloods.

Red-blooded Trace hadn't been invited—surprise! He guessed Charles thought that was some kind of insult, but he figured he'd breathe a lot better without being around the stench of way-too-expensive aftershave and even-more-expensive entitlement.

When the guard gave them instructions for how to

reach the meeting room, Trace got into the elevator and rode up to the twentieth floor with his friends. But he was just as glad to stay in the hallway, still around the corner from the suite that Charles had commandeered for this face-to-face. Hanging behind. Keeping watch.

That didn't make him a coward, did it? It made him first line of attack, unless Charles had an ambush set up in the conference suite. And Dillon Charles was the kind of guy who liked to keep his own hands clean.

"Wish us luck," whispered Mitch as he and Smith turned the corner.

Trace just snorted. He wasn't even sure what "luck" would look like, here—except for everyone getting out in one piece. It wasn't likely Charles and his crowd would threaten Smith and Mitch with real violence, exiles or not. But you never could tell.

One thing he'd learned over his decade as a secret society misfit was that what people said the rules were, and how they actually behaved, weren't always the same thing. Hell, they were hardly ever the same thing. Usually, the rules just provided a way for jerks to rationalize their jerkiness.

Only a few months back, one young, hotheaded Comitatus had taken it on himself to stab a member of the inner circle—Arden's father. So, no. Despite Charles' veneer of civilization in setting up this official conclave, not even Smith and Mitch trusted the guy to keep his word.

Trace waited. He folded his arms. After a while, he unfolded his arms, and his healing ribs still felt tender. In the imaginary paintball fight Smith had described, he'd now lost to the reds and yellows instead of the purples and browns.

And he'd lost Sibyl.

Trace wished he knew what to do about that. He'd tried leaving messages for her, but she never called him back. He'd even gone by her condo, only to have the door answered by a middle-aged yuppie with a golfer's tan. Luckily, Trace had hesitated, torn between fear that this might be Sibyl's new lover and confusion that maybe this was her dad, long enough to *not* damage the guy before learning that he was neither. The condo's owner had never heard of Sibyl. Or Isabel. Or anyone matching her description. And no, he hadn't hired anyone to house-sit while he was out of the country.

Could Trace have dreamed her? And if he had, couldn't he have dreamed a less complicated woman?

Now, waiting in the hallway of the downtown Dallas high-rise, he shifted his weight on the plush carpet. He checked his phone, in case Sibyl had called. Nothing. He strained to hear any kind of commotion from the meeting rooms, fairly sure that either Smith or Mitch could yell loud enough to get his attention if they needed him. Nothing.

Damn. Even if he came across as desperate, he had to try calling Sibyl again. He had to know that she was okay. Trace pressed the speed dial button he'd set for her.

A ringtone version of LeAnn Rimes' "Right Kind of Wrong" played out from behind him.

He spun. And there she stood, just outside the door to the stairs, blinking at him like she had even less idea what to say than he did. *Sibyl.* She looked good—better than he remembered, which was saying something, though maybe the fact that she'd bled on him had colored his memory. She wore jeans for once, probably because December had arrived, and an oversize shirt, although he wondered what wouldn't look oversize on a little slip like her. Her long brown hair threatened to curtain off her face from the rest of the world. Her big eyes, and that solemn, taking-everything-too-seriously expression...

Torn between diving at her to scoop her into a hard hug, versus snarling the first insult he could think of just to show that she hadn't hurt him, Trace stared. He also shut his phone.

Her own phone stopped ringing, even as she dug it out of her pocket and, with a single beep, seemed to silence it.

"Hey," he said finally. Good. Noncommital.

Sibyl looked down at the carpet, then back up. Most women would have smiled at that point, just to be polite. She stayed solemn. "Hi."

"So..." God, he hoped she'd enjoyed their time in bed together as much as he had, because he sure as hell wasn't going to win her over with his sparkling conversation. "What...?"

"How long have they been in there?" she asked, seeming to find her purpose again. She strode by him, glanced around the corner. "The meeting. I wanted to listen in."

About a dozen questions crowded his head. Somehow, the one that slipped out first was, "How'd you even know about it?"

"Greta. She overheard some of the planning about the Schmomitatus."

Oh, yeah. Since Greta's father had been a member of the society, before his long-ago exile, they'd relaxed some of their vigilance around her—especially Mitch. How someone as chatty as Mitch had ever taken a vow of secrecy with a straight face, Trace couldn't figure.

"So why do you want to listen?"

"Because I need to know."

"It would be a lot safer to wait until we get back to Greta's and ask us then. So where…"

But Sibyl's examination of the walls distracted him. She said, "Don't trust them."

"Smith and Mitch?"

"Any of them." Including him? That would explain a lot. But before he could ask her about that, she seemed to find what she was seeking. She dragged a cushioned chair over to the hallway wall, then stood on it and began to work on—oh. A wall vent. She used a Swiss Army knife to remove the screws, then lifted down a vent cover, careful not to make noise. The way she bent, so incredibly low, to brace the vent cover against the chair beneath her feet, was poetry. Then, stretching back up to grasp the edge of the resulting shaft with her hands and placing one booted foot on the back of the chair, she readied to boost herself upward.

In two steps, Trace caught her by the hips and lifted her well away, to the floor, instead. "Are you crazy?"

Her eyes flashed anger at the word, but all she said was, "I need to hear them."

"By crawling through vents?"

"They'd see me if I just opened the door and leaned in."

He hated the sarcastic edge he heard or imagined in her statement—the unspoken *duh*. So he wasn't a genius like her, or even as educated as his once wealthy friends. But he had good survival instincts. So he put on his meanest face and loomed over her, as threatening as possible—pretty easy, considering their different heights—and snarled, "It's dangerous."

To his amazement, shy little Sibyl of the Faline eyes glared right back up at him, not at all cowed. "So's cage fighting."

"I'm good at cage fighting."

"And I'm good at sneaking!" She was? "But anything connected to the Comitatus is dangerous. So was setting up a blind meeting with Arden."

"Yeah. You almost got flattened by a train."

"But I didn't!" Which is when something shifted in her gaze, something he hadn't expected. She didn't look any more frightened than she had before, just more... soft. "You were there."

Her near miss with the train had scared the hell out of him then and he didn't even know her! Now that he'd developed some kind of complicated feelings for Sibyl, remembering it made him dizzy. "And now—"

But she stopped him with soft fingers over his angry mouth. "You're here now, too."

And she smiled.

And Trace lost track of his argument.

* * *

Sibyl could barely breathe past the clicking into place of puzzle pieces…but for once, this wasn't about solving an equation or answering a Comitatus-based riddle. This was significantly more…immediate. This was about Trace. She'd run from him, back at her first meeting with Arden, and nearly been killed. A few days ago, she'd run again, but not because she feared him, exactly—because she'd feared his connection to his bloodline, his…masculinity. The masculinity that had given her more pleasure than she could remember.

It had felt like a betrayal. The history of masculinity really was one of violence and domination and competition and conquest…. And protection. When one was truly lucky, when the man was truly decent. And some men had to be decent. Her father had been.

Sibyl felt the surprising pull in her cheeks as she smiled up at Trace, her lover. Her champion. "You're here. Please boost me up."

He blinked down at her, and she lay her hand over his heart, felt its thrumming beneath her fingertips. Life. Future? "Please?"

When he continued to hesitate, she turned from him and stepped back onto the chair—champion or not, he couldn't be allowed to keep her from finishing her previous quest. And could she finish it? A sudden wash of optimism suggested she could.

Then, behind her, he spanned her hips with his hands and lifted, kicking the chair out of the way from beneath her so that he could stand closer to the wall. "Fine!"

She drew her feet up and used the platform of his

shoulders to stand, to insert herself into the square metal tunnel. She wished she could smile down at him again—she, who used to go so long between smiles. But the vent didn't give enough room to turn around, so she simply waved a blind hand behind her.

She hadn't expected the warm, calloused touch that brushed her fingers, but she appreciated it more than she could've anticipated. Her champion…

No distractions. Knowledge is power.

Refocusing, Sibyl began to shimmy her way through the venting, her fingers quickly caking with grit, her face brushing the occasional cobweb. For a fancy building, its vents sure were dusty. She tried to hold her breathe, pausing only to breath through her sleeve or her collar when she had to. When she reached a small intersection, she turned toward the faint thrum of male voices.

Of course she recognized Mitch's voice first. Mitch Talbott was a talker, relating their last few months with the area Comitatus. "…pretty much how it all went down. Smith's dad seems to be head of the local powers, not that he has anything to do with us, 'cause…hello? Exiled? Greta and Arden know the menfolk are up to something, but as long as we keep them safe, they're happy to stop asking questions."

Hardly, thought Sibyl, wondering if Mitch was lying or if he honestly believed his report.

"And what of Isabel Daine?" demanded Dillon Charles. He sounded different than he had nearly a decade earlier at the prep school where her scholarship, and her father's willingness to work there, had once promised an unparalleled future. His voice sounded deeper. But he'd gotten older, too. "We attended the same classes at the academy. The coincidence troubles me."

The fact that you aren't telling them how your father and Trace's—that is, Judge LaSalle—railroaded me is also troubling, thought Sibyl, squirming just a little bit closer before stopping. The vents allowed her a partial view of the man from above.

"Wait." That was Smith's voice. "How old is she?"

"Like I know? She was pretty young, then. She'd skipped some classes, thought being some kind of prodigy meant she deserved our level of education."

She'd once been impressed by his wealth and position. She'd even imagined some kind of Cinderella story, she from a lower-middle-class family being courted by the prince of New Orleans.

Except that she'd been stupid.

"Well, she's just a little, lonely thing." Mitch dismissed her that easily. "Someone Greta took in. She can't be any threat to the Comitatus, right?"

"Except that she's an arsonist!"

Sibyl's gut clenched. So this was how it would come out?

"And worse," Dillon continued, "she's a killer."

Chapter 9

Thank heavens Sibyl had learned to lay low in jail. Her instinct, like that of any prey animal, was to freeze until the danger passed.

Otherwise, she might have launched herself bodily through the vent cover and tried to prove Dillon right. The killer part, anyway.

"In fact," he mused beneath her, "didn't your friend Greta Kaiser have a fire, sometime after she took in Isabel?"

A fire the Comitatus—one deranged member, at least—had started. Surely the others would remember that. She felt sick.

It was Mitch who laughed first, his mirth like bass music. "Sibyl?"

"So she's changed her name, too?" insisted Dillon. "Little Sibyl's a murderer?"

"I said a killer," Dillon clarified—the son of a lawyer, probably a lawyer himself by now, he would certainly know the technical difference. "She was imprisoned for arson and manslaughter—of her own father!"

That cut off Mitch's amusement mid-laugh. "Imprisoned?"

"Her father," repeated Smith, more slowly. That was Smith's *I'm starting to figure things out* voice. Sibyl, unsure she wanted him to figure anything out at all, hated that voice.

"If you care for Greta Kaiser—and as she's of the blood, I can hardly blame you—you will let her know what kind of element she has allowed into her home. You will protect her from that kind of element. And if you have any respect left for your own bloodline, your own history, you will stay on guard against the girl's too-coincidental appearance. You can hardly expect the society to help you, if you're providing aid to its enemies."

"So Sibyl's not of the blood herself?" Smith had definitely been thinking about Sibyl way more than she would have liked. She should probably take the fact that he'd considered her "of the blood" as a compliment to how much she'd learned about the society—instead of wanting to barf.

"Hardly. Her father was the hired help!"

Security guard.

"Well, we'd sure hate to help our fathers' enemies." That was Mitch, sounding way too serious for Mitch... which gave Sibyl some hope that he was still playing a role. "Why do you think we're here, telling you about Trace's sword?"

To get information, supposedly. Sibyl tried to swallow past the sick lump still wedged in her throat. Part of her just wanted to flee—to grab Trace and drag him out of here before his friends told him who and what she really was, or at least Dillon Charles' version thereof. If she could just keep him from learning how stupid she'd once been, and how badly her time in jail had broken her, maybe he would continue to kiss her, hold her, protect her the way he'd been doing recently. But she'd only been in love with Trace…

…love?…

…for a few days, perhaps a few weeks. She'd needed to learn the truth about her father's death—to avenge that death—for almost a decade. She still needed to do so. She had to finish loving one good man, her daddy, before she could trust herself to try loving another.

So she lay there in the confines of the ventilation duct, lump in her throat and gut full of acid, and listened as Trace's friends changed the subject and drew the needed information out of Dillon Charles.

"Do you know what this is?" asked Dillon, after Mitch had handed over the photographs.

"I'm no expert," qualified Mitch. "But I'm guessing… some kind of bladed weapon? Give me a minute…not a spear. Not an ax, but that's closer…"

"This is an early medieval sword." So Dillon knew his stuff when it came to weapons. Big surprise. "I need you to get this for me."

"Whoa there." Even if she couldn't glimpse Smith's

smile—and she could, if barred by the ventilation grille—Sibyl would have heard the charm oozing from his voice. "Not so fast. Why would we do that?"

"Did exile rob you two of all your honor? He *stole* it!"

"From his grandfather's bungalow. I'm not saying I approve—" nor that he didn't "—but how does your claim to the sword trump his? I mean, sure, Trace is baseborn and all. And he's exiled like us," added Smith, still with suspicious charm, "but…his grandfather. Not yours."

"Except that this sword belongs in the Comitatus."

"Because…?"

"Because it's one of the hero's blades!" insisted Dillon.

"Blades? Plural?" As if Smith didn't have the sword of Aeneas hidden back at Greta's place.

"It's a Comitatus matter," hedged Dillon. "You two…"

"Didn't bring the bad influence with us," Smith finished, nudging the conversation back in his direction. "We get it, Dillon. We're exiles. You think we can forget that? We've got to face that mistake every day of our lives. We've paid, and we'll keep on paying, and, well, we probably deserve it."

Smith turned away from his one-time cohort. Getting a full-on look at his expression, Sibyl marveled at his ability to lie—and she knew he was lying. All he needed was a melodramatic piano background to complete the scene. Regret leaving the secret society? She didn't doubt it. But deserve that exile and admit it?

Not likely.

Dillon didn't burst out laughing, the way she'd feel tempted to if she weren't swallowing back roiling horror at the earlier conversation. So Smith continued. "Bad enough to have lost our money, our work, our homes. But you know what's worse?"

"So much worse," echoed Mitch, pushing it.

"It's knowing that we betrayed our lineage. Our fathers and our fathers' fathers. Our history. The one solace we have is knowing that, at least, we can't lose. Where we come from. What's in our blood.

"You want the sword? Part of me understands. It's probably better off with you, with someone who's legitimately of the blood. And at least it's given us this one chance to connect, to, I guess, to visit this world. Just for a while."

"Despite our sins," added Mitch. He shouldn't. He didn't have Smith's gift for bull—even when serious, Mitch generally sounded like he was joking. But something Trace's friends said, as over-the-top as Sibyl found it, must have resonated with Dillon so powerfully that he missed that.

"We've got a piece of Comitatus history, right?" Smith urged. "It'll be hard enough to give it up, because it's maybe the last thing we have, but maybe if you could explain. If we knew what we were returning."

Dillon sighed—but nodded. "Of course you know that we're descended from heroes."

"Is the Pope Catholic?" countered Mitch. "Is the sky blue? Do Stuarts live in big mansions?"

And—Sibyl heard something else. Faintly. From behind her.

From Trace. But…she had to hear *this*.

"One summer during college, I had the privilege of seeing the Comitatus archives in New Orleans and I found a list. Not just heroes—Charlemagne and El Cid and King Arthur—but their swords. As if their swords had been members of the Comitatus, too, you know? The papers even showed which family line descended from which hero, maybe still had which sword."

Smith looked even less convinced than was Sibyl. "Wouldn't the families already know it?"

"Except that the swords became obsolete. A century or so after gunpowder became common, groups like the musketeers replaced knights and swords seemed downright archaic. Most families kept their swords, but the men weren't bringing them to meetings anymore. They were shoved aside, like inkpots or candle-snuffers."

"Or vinyl records," mourned Mitch. When the other two looked at him askance, he frowned back. "Hey, when CDs came out, people were tossing their turntables. Now vinyl's cool again."

Dillon didn't concede the example. "The thing is, gunpowder became too common. Vulgar, even. Anybody, of any class, can pull a trigger and discharge a pistol. It takes training to properly wield a blade. But by the time the Comitatus saw that…"

"By then, the swords weren't community property anymore," finished Smith.

"But the idea behind them was. Have either of you heard of the *noblesse d'épée?*"

Nobles of the sword? translated Sibyl to herself, even as Dillon spoke the words out loud.

"The term refers to the old nobility in France," he continued. "The classical nobles. The chivalrous nobles. The fighting nobles."

Only Sibyl saw Mitch, behind Dillon, pump his fist and mouth something that looked like, Go, Fighting Nobles! Like a team mascot.

"The Comitatus descend from the *noblesse d'épée,*" explained Dillon. "I haven't been able to get back into the archives since, but once I get that sword back, I can make a case to the higher-ups. How powerful would it be to bring those swords together? To remind everyone how special we are? Maybe to help support Phil Stuart over his cousin for position of overlord?"

Sibyl tried to concentrate on the Comitatus conversation—the admission that they had archives in New Orleans was, itself, the most important thing she'd learned in years! But other voices, including Trace's fought for dominance. Trying to follow both felt like listening to post-modern music.

Trace's voice, faint through the labyrinthine ventilation ducts, triumphed. "I said *stay where you are!*"

Which he was clearly saying to someone else, someone Sibyl didn't know about—but which, she suspected, carried a message for her, too. Because Trace wasn't scared of anybody or anything.

Except maybe of her getting hurt.

Below her, in the borrowed boardroom, Dillon was

talking about how his family had descended from Charlemagne and how Trace's great-grandfather must have been keeping the sword for them. How the Judge could best sort everything out. But Sibyl couldn't concentrate.

Damn it!

With answers at her fingertips, Sibyl began to crawl awkwardly backward, toward what was increasingly sounding like a scuffle from the foyer near the elevators. She banged an elbow on the air shaft's side—twice. The corner proved especially tight, but she could also better hear the sounds of someone hitting a wall, someone grunting in pain.

She hurried.

She caught her shirt on a sharp, loose screw, but a wedged hand managed to unhook it. Finally, continuing backward, she made it to the point where—

Her feet touched the vent cover.

Trace had locked her in?

He had. But she didn't feel trapped. She felt protected.

Now the fight sounds were unmistakable through the vent cover—not the *whack!* Or *pow!* of movies, but the real, almost silent thuds of flesh on flesh, grunts of someone struggling for a choke hold. She knew the sounds from her years in prison…and from watching Trace fight.

Trace. He really could take care of himself. But she could tell he was up against more than one person. And she'd long ago stopped believing in fair fights. Without another thought, Sibyl kicked the vent loose with both feet and pushed herself out of the crawlway, dropping to land lightly, ready to join him.

From the dazed expression on Trace's face, where he slumped against the wall—and to judge from the three bodies sprawled around him, two more still standing—she'd made it just in time.

Trace had done everything he could to protect her. He'd set the vent cover lightly in place, in case someone passed by, to hide her route. When he heard the elevator ding open, he'd shifted to the opposite wall to draw attention—just in case.

He'd figured a little paranoia never hurt. Not with Sibyl at stake.

Turned out he'd had cause for every extra precaution. Five toughs stalked around the corner and down the carpeted corridor toward him like a gang, full of threat and bravado.

Why the hell that surprised him, he couldn't figure. He wasn't like Mitch, or even Smith, thinking the Comitatus types had any grasp of real honor. He'd known Dillon Charles on and off for years, after being acknowledged by the Judge, and heard firsthand how selective that honor could be even for the true believers.

For example, the guys approaching him were defi-nitely *not* Comitatus types. Their sagging jeans and faded shirts were thrift store, not Brooks Brothers. That meant they wouldn't have to follow any annoying rules about how people "of the blood" should be treated, even if Trace still counted. But they'd had to get into the building, and know which floor to target, somehow. This was no coincidence.

Dillon, of course. Delegating dishonor to keep his hands clean. Which, to Trace, wasn't honor at all.

"Hey," he'd grunted, as if they were just passing by.

But they'd surrounded him. "Big," said the guy in front, with a shaved head and raggedy denim jacket. But he wasn't talking to Trace. "Dark. Yeah, this is the guy."

Not with Sibyl here, damn it.

"The guy telling you to stay back," Trace warned, mostly for Sibyl's benefit. God forbid she come back into the middle of a fight. Hadn't he endangered her enough? Just to be sure, he added, "I said, stay where you are."

Very loudly. He hoped she heard him and obeyed.

The five who'd come here to punish him for trespassing on hallowed ground grinned. They thought he was scared. He wasn't—except for Sibyl.

When the first one, a lieutenant to his left, lunged, Trace showed them just how scared he wasn't. *Wham!* A simple body check, with the kind of force that should have echoed down the hallway, took the lieutenant down. Probably temporary, but it felt great all the same. It also bought time for Trace to turn and—

Yes! Shoulder block lowlife #2.

That, unfortunately, is when they all piled onto him at once, and he lost track of who was who. All he knew was the bloodlust, the brutality, the joy of releasing his big body to do what it did best. *One* of the things it did best.

Destroy.

He knew he probably couldn't win this one. The odds just weren't with him. But the choreography of the fight almost delighted him, in a feral kind of way. The beautiful arc of blood against the papered wall, when he caught Baldy in the nose. The *oof!* of one guy with a prison tat across his cheek when Trace flipped him backward onto the plush carpet and landed on top of him, full weight. The sense of almost flying, when he rolled off that one in time to catch another, hard on the chin with his head, as he stood again. The crack of a bone here. The grunt of lost breath there. Even the tooth-shaking crash as he hit the wall, as one head shot too many sent him reeling. It had a vibrancy to it. Fancy rules about honor and secret societies, those felt like make-believe. But this was flesh, blood, bone. Real. No pain. Just exhilaration.

Until, through the swooping, spinning effect of near unconsciousness, Trace saw the vent cover pop off the wall. *No.* He saw two little, cowboy-booted feet slide out, and he wanted to shout, *"No! Stay where you are!"* But he couldn't let these thugs know she was there. Instead, he somehow gathered the strength to sweep the legs out from under Baldy. Again. So what if Baldy kicked him for it. What was another pound to an elephant?

But then the weirdest thing happened, so weird that he must be imagining it. He must be unconscious already.

Because the grace with which little Sibyl landed on the carpeted floor, across from him, was one thing.

But the sight of her suddenly leaping, landing on Baldy's back, riding him to the carpeted floor and knocking him out with a well-placed heel of her palm to the nose. The sight of her almost levitating off him, spinning like a dancer in time to elbow the second fighter in the ribs, doubling him over before kneeing him in the groin, then the head....

That was another sight entirely.

Another guy Trace had taken down, the one he'd thought of as the lieutenant, had climbed back up the wall until he was standing. He staggered toward Sibyl. She turned toward him, completely outsized and not the least bit cowed. She looked downright belligerent. And Trace finally gave up his fight against the darkness of unconsciousness.

He wasn't scared for her anymore.

"Come on, Trace." Sibyl patted his whiskery cheeks, pet back his dark hair. He was breathing—she'd almost lost the ability to breathe herself, until she'd recognized that. He had a strong pulse. But it still terrified her, seeing the big man laid out like this. "Please, Trace. Wake up. I don't want anyone to find us here like this."

He groaned. That didn't encourage her too much. Groaning had kind of replaced exhaling, for him.

Bastards, she thought—then felt guilty for using that particular epithet. But still.

"Trace? Someone else is going to come soon. Wake up." She held his head in her lap and stroked his rough cheek, amazed by his vulnerability. Especially after having seen the damage he'd inflicted on the lowlifes she assumed were Dillon Charles' goons. Not a bad combination. Not something she'd ever considered, in a man.

To her immense relief, Trace's eyes slid open. He squinted against the overhead lights—good. His pupils contracting, and the same size…she'd read enough to know just how good that was.

"Hey," he rasped up at her.

"Hey, there," she whispered back, and kissed him. Right there. Surrounded by five wounded, unconscious men. His lips felt like she'd remembered—strong. Soft. His cheek felt scratchy and familiar against hers. She hated to pull away, but she hadn't spent a decade hiding behind survival instincts just to ignore them now. So she drew back, holding his big hand in hers as she did.

"Did you just…?" He levered himself up on his elbows, squinting his confusion at the litter of bodies around them.

Damn. She'd hoped he wouldn't notice. Yes, she'd taken down the last two lowlifes. She'd do it again, if she saw Trace lying there like that, helpless and beaten.

It wasn't like he hadn't already hurt them before she even got there.

The question in his dark gaze held undertones of awe…and of uncertainty. While she would have liked to explore the awe, the uncertainty concerned her. Once his friends left the conference room, Trace would learn just how tough a background Sibyl had. She didn't want him to suspect her. She wanted him to protect her as his own damsel in distress.

So she made a face, as if to say, *What could you possibly mean?*

"Wake up," she insisted. "We have to get out of here now. Can you walk?"

"Um…yeah. Sure." He needed a few tries to stand. At one point Sibyl almost crumpled under the weight of him using her shoulder as a brace. But he managed it and, with her struggling to help support him under one of his arms, they made it to the elevator together.

Other than a few grunts, and whistling breath through his teeth, Trace stayed silent as she got them off on the second floor, then began moving deeper into the building. Then, probably more from pain than curiosity, he asked, "Where…?"

"There's another stairway, toward the back. We can take that exit and avoid the security guards asking questions." Why did she feel like she was somehow insulting her father's memory every time she found a way around a security guard? She'd done it often enough.

"How'd…?"

"I hacked into the building schematics when I learned the meeting was going to be here, then checked out which room Dillon reserved. That's how I knew about the vent."

But he was shaking his head, pulling back from her to brace himself against a glass wall. Even with him hurt, she was no match for his strength. She had to let go, had to endure him staring down at her while he caught his breath.

"How," he tried again, "did you learn to fight like that?"

Damn. She'd thought he'd been out. "Like what?"

Trace narrowed his eyes. Sibyl widened hers and tried

to look especially Faline-esque. She could see when the uncertainty crept into his expression, when he began to doubt his perceptions. Then she felt guilty.

But also relieved.

"Come on," she urged, again. The momentary rest had done him good; he could hobble with her, instead of using her as a too-small crutch. Somehow they made it down the steps, to the back exit and through the emergency door.

The alarms went off, but one quick corner and they'd joined the crowds in Thanks-Giving Square, well away from the Comitatus's immediate reach. Let Mitch and Smith deal with the alarm, and with that double-crossing Dillon Charles.

"You really didn't fight those other two guys?" asked Trace once more, after they'd climbed onto a southward-bound bus.

Three, actually. One of the ones you took out regained consciousness.

"Don't be silly," Sibyl chided. But she also leaned— carefully, so as not to hurt him—into his big, warm, solid side. He even made a public bus palatable. When his arm lifted awkwardly around her, she closed her eyes and breathed him in, and fell more deeply into both love and despair.

It wouldn't be long before Trace learned, from his friends, exactly where Sibyl had learned to fight…and just how badly she'd misrepresented herself, just how tainted she'd become.

She might as well enjoy his simple, honest affection while she could. So she snuggled up against him, watching the city street with its Christmas-decorated cafés and banks flow past.

"I thought I saw you…" He pushed once more, though more gently.

"Maybe you imagined it," she lied, almost voice-lessly.

But she might not have been talking about the fight.

Chapter 10

Trace hadn't imagined it. The longer he remained conscious—arguing with Sibyl against going to an emergency room, making the exchanges to other buses to get back to Greta's neighborhood—the surer he became.

Little Sibyl, helpless Sibyl, shy Sibyl, could kick butt.

Damn, that was sexy. But her lying about it worried him. He'd thought he was getting to know her, but maybe he didn't know her at all. That thought gave him an odd ache that felt different from the physical fallout of his own fight.

"What the hell?" Smith hurried down the tree-lined, litter-strewn block from Greta's to meet them, as they hiked home from the station, and inserted himself under one of Trace's arms. That *was* a lot easier than struggling not to put his weight on little Sibyl. "You actually walked away from that? I had Arden calling hospitals!"

"Note to self." Mitch slid under Trace's other arm. Sibyl, who hadn't complained once all the way from downtown Dallas, backed away to make room. "Stay on Trace's good side, or else."

"I'll…" Sibyl kept on backing up toward the train station. "I'll just…"

"Don't go." For once, Trace tried to look his most bedraggled and pitiful. It helped that talking used too much air needed for breathing, so his words came out in grunts.

She hesitated on the chilly sidewalk.

His friends exchanged dark glances he maybe wasn't supposed to notice.

"I couldn't…find you before," Trace insisted, wincing as they started walking again. He noted that Smith's girlfriend, Arden, waited on the porch, concerned. Public transit really did take longer than driving home. But he pivoted his head to try to hold Sibyl's gaze. "I didn't… like it."

Sibyl shut her eyes—then opened them, decided and nodded.

Thank God for small favors.

Apparently his friends had called in the cavalry— what cavalry they had left, with so little money or influence. Actually, it wasn't a bad effort. Beautiful Arden Leigh opened the door for them on the porch. Once they made it into Greta's faded old foyer, Arden's sturdier, Latina friend, Val, stepped in to take over for Mitch under Trace's arm.

"We should check him out downstairs," Val noted. She had to be the most practical, guy-like woman Trace had ever met. "In case we need to take him to an emergency room."

"Nope," announced Trace, leaning his considerable weight toward the stairs. "No emergency rooms. Bed."

"You say that now, but you could be in shock," Val argued. Trace wondered if maybe she had more experience with beatings than anyone else in the room. Trust fund fellows like Smith and Mitch didn't exactly rumble or anything.

"I've been…in fights…" Damn, he wished he could talk better. Day after tomorrow would be the worst, but he could walk—with effort. He could breathe. He didn't feel dizzy, and his vision was good. "Sibyl?"

Too many people crowded around him in the too-small space, and he couldn't see her. He began to tense. "Sib!"

"His pupils are equal and responsive," she announced from somewhere behind him. Good. She hadn't left. "He hasn't lost consciousness since one point during the fight. He can walk on his own. It just…hurts him. He's been in fights before. He knows his own body."

Trace grinned in her general direction—he was pretty sure he hadn't lost any teeth in the fight to make that scary—and let the others help him up the narrow stairs, get him to his bed, pull his T-shirt up over his head and off his arms.

"Madre de Dios," whispered Val.

"Your bruises have been breeding," explained Mitch

in awe, while Trace laid back on the bed with a sigh of relief. That felt better, if not good. "They've given birth to new, super-colorful offspring. I don't want to adopt any."

Trace shrugged, painful or not. They'd be a lot more colorful tomorrow.

For a while, everything focused on first aid basics: a bag of frozen peas on his black eye and a few more frozen vegetables on his ribs and gut. Ibuprofen would help the pain and swelling—after he'd insisted that he wasn't bleeding internally, that he'd know if he was bleeding internally. Comfrey poultices from Greta eventually to replace the ice after ten minutes. Trace couldn't remember the last time he'd gotten this kind of care after a fight…especially not after he'd lost this badly.

That, and the thought of the kind of girls who prowled the no-holds-barred competitions, turned on by the damage, made him turn his head on the pillow and look at Sibyl.

She sat beside him on his bed, leaning against the headboard, solemnly watching the others fuss over him. When he couldn't find her, this last week, he'd considered all kinds of reasons she might have gone. Was she that freaked out by blood? Or had his lovemaking somehow scared her off? Maybe it was disgust over his fighting.

She didn't look disgusted, now. Considering how well she'd fought, he wasn't surprised. Worried about why she kept lying about it, yeah. Curious what else he didn't know about her. But not surprised.

She didn't look disgusted, but she sure as hell looked upset. In that solemn, private way of hers, anyhow.

"So, Dillon Charles wants the sword," Mitch relayed, if only to keep Trace's mind off the pain. "No duh, right? He thinks it might belong to his family, if it's the sword of Charlemagne."

Sibyl had named Charlemagne as a possible owner of the ancient blade. She also didn't seem to like the guy. That should be enough for him to rid himself of the damned thing—he didn't want anything to do with the Comitatus, damn it! He didn't want to upset Sibyl further.

So why did the idea of handing over the sword make his gut twist worse than the beating he'd taken? Even now, when he glanced toward where he'd laid it—now safely wrapped in a towel—on the bureau top, his first instinct was the word, the absolute certainty, *mine*.

"He found a list once, in the New Orleans archives, of what swords go with what families," Mitch continued, but Smith warned, *"Mitch."*

"He thinks finding them would give the, er, Schmomitatus a kind of focus to reclaim our—their—position as the Fightin' Nobles."

"Mitch!" Now Smith glared, first at his friend, then at Sibyl and at the other ladies—Greta and Arden and Val—closer to the doorway, where they could go get more ice, or ibuprofen, or bandages. "Ladies, my apologies, but could we have some privacy?"

Smith never had liked Mitch's habit of calling their old society "the Schmomitatus" as a shortcut to get around their vows of secrecy. Trace went back and forth, himself. On the one hand, screw the Comitatus. On the other hand, a promise was a promise. Right?

Still, he hated to send Sibyl away. He liked her presence beside him. So he felt relieved when she didn't make a move to leave.

He felt less relieved when, practically vibrating with stress, Sibyl said, "You can let them *all* know."

"Know what?" asked Trace, suddenly suspicious that he didn't want to. Know, that is.

Especially when Sibyl looked directly at him and said, "Dillon told them who I am. He told them about the years I spent in prison. He told them I'm a killer."

There. She'd said it. No going back.

Trace barked out a laugh—but maybe something in her expression smothered it almost immediately. Then he just stared at her.

Say something, pleaded Sibyl silently. *Please say something.*

The others said plenty, in that endless stretching of uncertainty. Greta said, "Poor thing," and Arden half moaned a protest of, "No!" Val, who knew Sibyl's self-defense abilities, murmured, "That explains a lot." Mitch said, "Okay, now that's just eerie. How'd she know that?"

Smith rolled his eyes—"She eavesdropped, doofus."

And still Trace said nothing. He had nothing to say to her. He didn't like her anymore. He couldn't stand to look at her—except, he *was* looking at her, studying her. His bruised face, raw along one jaw, held more confusion than condemnation.

Still, the first words he spoke, he was still staring at her. "Get out."

No... Sibyl shut her eyes, surprised that the movement sent hovering tears down her cheek. But as she shifted to move back, Trace—with a grunt of pain—caught her wrist gently. His hands could break bones, but not hers. He turned his gaze to the others, to brook no confusion. "Get out and leave us alone."

"Look," said Smith. "I'm sure there's—"

Trace growled low in his throat.

Smith let Arden pull him after the others, shutting the door behind him, leaving her alone with the man she'd only hours ago thought of as her champion.

She met his gaze far more steadily than she felt. She wasn't sure she could speak, though.

Luckily, he could, releasing her wrist as he did. "That's ridiculous."

What?

"You're no killer."

"What if you're wrong?"

He snorted. "I'm not."

He looked blurry now. Was she crying? She hadn't cried so much since her daddy died. "You're not," she agreed, smiling as he brushed the tears off her cheek with a rough thumb and a caught breath—it still hurt him some to move. So he wouldn't have to strain himself, she settled farther down on the bed to his level, face to face on the pillow. The bed smelled of him. Of safety. "But I was convicted of it anyway."

"So talk to me. What went down?"

"My real name—my first name—was Isabel."

And for the first time, Sibyl told her story to a willing listener. An accepting listener. One who even, maybe cared about her, more than her past. With every detail, she felt a horrible, stagnant weight falling off her and vanishing, and the bond between her and Trace growing.

She explained the skipped grades and the scholarship to the same academy Dillon Charles attended—"I knew you were smart, but *damn,*" murmured Trace. She told him how her father took a job doing night security at the school. Then she described the horror of her father's death in a fire, the Kafka-esque nightmare of finding herself accused and convicted of both arson and manslaughter. And somehow, it didn't hurt as much as it used to. The memories felt diluted, worn out by overuse. The tragedy had happened almost half a lifetime ago.

For her.

Trace, on the other hand, looked increasingly ill, even before he learned that his biological father was the judge who'd convicted her. She traced a finger up and down the hard curve of his naked shoulder, hoping the mere contact would assure him that she didn't blame him. He was *not* his father's keeper.

"It didn't make sense," she explained softly, across the mere inches between their faces. "Not only wasn't it fair, but the conviction, the sentence—they didn't even make sense to the other girls in juvie. First, I tried solving my daddy's death myself, but no matter how good a hacker I became, I was still incarcerated. The police hadn't investigated much beyond the planted evidence. They figured I'd done it, the wrong element from way over on the working side of town, envious of what the rich folks had, not realizing my father was in the building. That's what they said."

Trace's haggard face, bruising on one cheekbone, scraped on the jaw, bristling with whiskers, had never looked so handsome as it did drinking in her explanation. His light eyes had dropped from her face, seeming to ache with her. *I love you,* she thought, and the thought delighted her.

But now wasn't exactly the time.

"So then I decided, if I couldn't find out who'd set the fire, I could find out why my mother and I had such a hard time getting counsel, and why the appeals courts were so set against me and, later, why I wasn't getting parole. I wasn't always a conspiracy theorist, you know. The Comitatus taught me to be. Because when I dug deep enough, I finally found them. Just because you're paranoid…"

Doesn't mean they aren't out to get you.

"And you never found out who set the fire?"

"No, but it's got to be Comitatus related, doesn't it? Why else would they work so hard to convict me? That's why I need to get into the archives in Louisiana that Dillon mentioned. They don't put some of that really important stuff into digital files, or I would have found it, I know I would. But if there are hard copy records on paper? Maybe they've got some information about it. What if I can find a way in, Trace? What if I can finally put all this behind me, and stop being such a…such a victim?"

When he lifted his eyes to hers, he looked sick. "I'll get you in."

"You know where it is?"

"Some secret rooms behind the old Arsenal—I'll find a way to get you in. I've just got to talk to the others, first."

Talk to them, and take her side. She felt sure of it! For the first time in over a decade, she knew she could count on someone. "Thank you," she whispered.

He blinked, somehow startled from his discomfort. Guilt over his dad, she supposed. Guilt over the role the Comitatus had played against her. But he wasn't Comitatus anymore, so that was okay, too.

Before she got off the bed, she closed those final inches between them and kissed him. Warm. Gentle. Real.

Hers.

Then she brushed his hair off his haggard face and went out to find the others—just outside the door.

"Oh, don't act so shocked," parried Smith, when she raised an eyebrow. "Like you don't do the same thing."

"You were talking too quietly," whispered Mitch, before following his friend in. "We didn't hear much."

She smiled at his kindness, let them shut the door between them—and, just as Smith had intimated, listened in. Old habits were hard to break and she couldn't wait to hear someone take her side, for once.

"She was framed," announced Trace's voice, just as she'd hoped.

"I know we all want to believe that—" started Smith, but Trace interrupted him.

"No, I *know* that. She was framed by the Comitatus. That's how she first found out about them. And we're going to get her into the New Orleans archives to make it up to her."

"I'm guessing Hallmark doesn't make a card for being framed so, sure," quipped Mitch. "Breaking her into secret Comitatus headquarters. Close second, right?"

"Wrong!" protested Smith. "I'm not saying that, if they're guilty, the New Orleans organization doesn't deserve some kind of comeuppance. But we took vows. Whether or not they're jerks, we aren't."

Trace said something Sibyl couldn't hear, but apparently his friends couldn't either, because he repeated himself. "I said, *I* am. Okay? No question they are, too—especially the Judge, and especially Dillon Charles. Either way, I need to fix this, with or without you two."

"Who are you," challenged Mitch, "and what have you done with the arrogant, testosterone-drenched side-of-meat who used to hang with us?"

Which is when Trace said, "I knew, okay?"

Outside the door, Sibyl frowned. *Knew what?*

The others clearly felt as confused. "Knew what?" demanded Smith.

"Dillon Charles used to be best friends with my brother. Half brother. The one who died before the Judge came to find me. He and my father stayed close. Neither of us liked it, but we spent time together, and he was always bragging about stuff."

"Stuff like…?"

Sibyl felt suddenly sick, as if the back of her mind was figuring out something the front didn't yet want to recognize.

"Like how there'd been this charity student at the academy he attended, and how he set a fire to get her thrown out. How nobody even looked his direction. Stuff like *that*. I figured he was just making it up, which was disgusting enough, you know? But it was real, he killed Sibyl's father, and Sibyl was sitting in jail doing time for it. I didn't know that part, that someone died, that the 'charity student' was convicted. But I knew enough, and I didn't do anything to help. I didn't turn him in because of some stupid code. So yeah. We're getting her into the Arsenal, so she can find proof and hopefully nail that son of a bitch to the wall."

And now she understood. She knew who'd killed her father, if not why. She understood why the Comitatus covered it up. And she understood her idiocy in trusting anyone with Comitatus blood—even Trace.

She'd thought he was different. And he was…marginally. He'd given up the benefits of life in the Comitatus. He'd disowned his biological father. But Trace's connection to that damned sword should have given her proof. He was still of that blood, of that world. He'd been just as likely to kick back and ignore the horrors that were being committed by the people of his class, just as the upper class of humankind had done for millennia.

She couldn't love that.

She could never love that.

Somehow, she managed to open the door without losing her control. "That's okay," she said, her voice barely shaking. "I don't need anyone's help."

Then she turned and walked out. The last thing she expected was the sound of Trace growling out a curse, then thundering after her.

His hand caught her elbow. "Wait!"

She spun on him. "I thought you were hurt."

"I am!" His set fists showed the truth of that. So did her memories of the last few hours. "Wait anyway."

She hesitated, torn between yanking free or ordering him back to bed. She shouldn't be torn. She shouldn't care.

But Sibyl had never been one to let something alone, had she? She couldn't make herself stop caring about Trace, anymore than she could have stopped herself from pursuing her father's killers.

She could, however, go back to lying about both. It was safer that way.

"Stay with your Comitatus friends. I'll do this alone."

"We aren't Comitatus! Not anymore."

"But you want to go back."

"I don't know what the hell I want!" He gripped the railing, pain even more clear around the outer edges of his eyes, the set of his jaw. "Except you."

"You can't have me!"

"To fix things with you."

She hesitated.

"Let me do this." Trace wasn't the kind of man who

could wheedle. It came out more like a command. "I want to be one of the good guys, here. For once. For you."

Sibyl stared up at him where he loomed over her, the word "alone" still echoing in her head. *Let me do this alone. I do everything alone.*

That was clearly how the world should work. Would always work. Despite this large, rugged man standing, half nude, in front of her, his fingers now very loose on her arm.

Every minute she spent with him now was just going to break her heart. But she could sacrifice her heart, if it finally led to the knowledge she needed—not just to understand.

The information, and opportunity, she needed to finally avenge herself and her poor, dead father.

So what if she broke her heart while getting it?

After she and Trace parted, she doubted she would ever need her heart again.

Chapter 11

Trace had never considered himself a planner. The fact that Smith and Mitch were willing to help him meant a lot. It just reminded him, yet again, that the guys who were born into the Comitatus didn't have to be jerks.

Not that he'd stay, even so. The pain of his healing bruises he could handle. They were almost an afterthought. The pain of not being able to help Sibyl? That, he wasn't sure he could stand.

"This is all about one thing," Smith explained, leaning over sheets of paper in the study at his girlfriend's big, Highland Park estate. They had all agreed that, after the attack during their earlier meeting, they couldn't risk keeping either the swords or themselves at Greta's house.

They'd made sure to carry both swords out during the middle of the day, when anyone who might be shadowing them—and surely Charles had paid someone to shadow them—might get good pictures of the assumed retreat. Now Sibyl, and Arden's former-cop friend, Val Diaz, were staying to protect the older lady.

All about one thing. *Sibyl,* thought Trace.

"The sword of Charlemagne," explained Smith, sliding a picture of Trace's sword across the table. "Dillon Charles wants that sucker. *Bad.* So we use that in the distraction."

Mitch made a wait-a-minute, clucking noise against his teeth. "He's not going to settle for a picture of it this time, no matter how much more convenient it'd be for us if he'd just give in and play stupid villain."

"No. We'll have to bring the real sword." Smith looked up at Trace. "Are you willing to risk losing it?"

Actually, he hated the idea of losing it. He wasn't sure why. It represented the society he'd come to hate. It had belonged to a conqueror who, according to Sibyl anyway, had had plenty of less-than-chivalrous moments as he forcibly converted much of Europe to Christianity. It had drawn Sibyl's own blood.

So why did he feel more honorable when he held it? More connected? Why did he continue to have dreams of himself with the sword, some kind of knight of old in valorous battle?

"Are you willing to risk it?" he asked Smith. His friend had been so excited about the possibilities of using the swords to reawaken the chivalry in other Comitatus members, men who hadn't irreparably lost their honor.

"I hate the idea, but it's your sword."

His friends really were his friends. They might give him grief over his rough ways or plain thinking, because, well…they were guys. But they didn't question his heritage. They'd never question his right to fight beside them.

They had set both swords, the flared sword of Aeneas and the long, straight sword of Charlemagne, on a sideboard. Trace looked at the medieval blade he'd pulled from his great-grandfather's rotting wall, as if it had called him to it. *Mine.*

But he'd been turning his back on his birthright his entire life. Why, with so much at stake, should he change now?

He looked up at Smith. "How do we use it to get Sibyl into the Arsenal archives?"

Smith grinned. "Honorably, of course."

"It's a trap," insisted Beckett Covington, Dillon's law intern and Comitatus mentee, as their town car pulled up to the Cabildo. The famed eighteenth-century capital house rose above New Orleans's Jackson Square in Old World elegance immediately beside the Saint Louis Cathedral. From the ground floor's arched gallery to the mansard roof, it had seen power come and go in this ancient city: French, then Spanish, then French, then finally American.

But the Comitatus hold on New Orleans—and, through it, the wider world—had never wavered, was never "gone." Here was the strength of a society that worked behind the scenes, a society based on bloodlines instead of mere nationalities.

"It's a trap," Beckett repeated when Dillon, not moving from the back seat, didn't first answer him. "People don't fight duels anymore."

But Beckett was young. Even here, where the Cabildo had been turned into a state museum, Beckett didn't yet understand how, when the Louisiana Purchase was signed on the second floor of this opulent mansion, Comitatus were there. When Louisiana seceded from the Union, Comitatus stood on both sides of the Great War, guarding a history far older than the United States itself.

"Perhaps people should fight duels." Dillon had been both wary and pleased to receive the hand-penned invitation from Smith Donnell—written in fountain pen on thick, hand-pressed parchment, as it should be. "The old ways had their justifications."

And he rose out of the town car to go face his destiny.

The museum might be closed for the evening, but appropriate workers had of course remained to open it up for them. Dillon, followed by Beckett, strode through the old state house with its gleaming floors and white walls as if he belonged here…which, of course, he did.

Beyond the pomp of the Cabildo lay the old Arsenal. For this, Dillon didn't need employees; he had the security codes to disarm and rearm the alarms. By entering the blockier, plainer building through the secret passage, Dillon was able to cross to the thick double doors of the main entrance and welcome his visitors as might a landlord.

Which, for the most part, he was.

The heavy door creaked as he pulled it open, the sound echoing through the large, empty first floor.

As requested—dictated, rather—Trace Beaudry and Smith Donnell had come alone. Good. Dillon wouldn't have put it past Beaudry to try to use this meeting as some sort of lowly ambush. But Dillon's faith in Smith, in the respect Smith still gave his father's ancient blood-lines, was rewarded. Nobody but the two men stood in the immediate shadow of the Arsenal, despite the tourists beyond.

Smith Donnell's shoulders hunched. Trace Beaudry, a half head taller than any of them, hulked sullenly.

"Please come in," invited Dillon.

Beaudry glared at him, but Smith responded with a nodded "Thank you." He could have belonged there, too, had he not forgotten his heritage and gotten himself exiled.

Smith…

Dillon would not have accepted even a note from outcast Trace Beaudry. Beaudry merited neither his concern, nor his honor, which is why Dillon had arranged some decidedly non-Comitatus thugs to teach him a lesson back in Dallas. Some people might have been impressed to find all five of those same thugs, beaten and in varying states of consciousness, sprawled outside the conference room. Mitch Talbott had whistled through his teeth.

But when Dillon had met Smith Donnell's gaze,

Smith's curled lip had mirrored his own disgust. One's competence in a low-class brawl hardly spoke for one's suitability as a noble. Dillon thought he'd recognized Smith's longing for what he'd abandoned. He, Dillon, had come so close to losing his own place of honor once. It made him uniquely sympathetic to Smith's plight.

Oh, he'd never welcome an exile back into the Comitatus fold, not without specific instructions from someone in the inner circle. Like that would ever happen! But he could do Smith the honor of a meeting, especially when Smith was willing to bring Beaudry here, to *his* territory.

According to the note, Beaudry—unwilling to part with his misbegotten sword of Charlemagne—might be convinced by one-on-one combat. And Smith was willing to second him, tending to the requirements of etiquette to make the duel happen. Right would be restored, and that particular thorn in Dillon's side removed.

And he would get his family sword!

Beaudry would likely have wanted Dillon to come to him. Beaudry, on his own, might not even know about the initial meeting the night before the duel, or about seconds. Beaudry probably thought he got to choose the form their fight would take.

Fisticuffs?

But with Smith on the side of the heroes, Dillon felt certain this one concession—arranging and then enacting a duel in the Comitatus-owned New Orleans Arsenal—would end the problem of Beaudry and the sword in the best possible way.

Especially with Beaudry in his territory now.

Where Dillon knew any thugs he might need. New Orleans was his rightful place. So was this building of ancient power.

"As the one challenged," Dillon said evenly, "I choose swords."

Act annoyed.

That's what Mitch and Smith had instructed Trace, the whole long drive from Texas. *He'll choose swords. Look upset.*

Yeah, Mitch had added, sounding less certain. *Like that.*

Because "annoyed" was kind of Trace's default expression. Having folded his big body into Mitch's latest car rebuild annoyed him. Being back in this blocky old Arsenal—the first floor of which he'd known since being drafted into the Comitatus himself—annoyed him, especially when he remembered how stupidly anxious he'd been to win his father's approval. Dillon Charles of the perfect tennis-and-Bahamas tan and too-expensive suits annoyed the snot out of him.

Worst of all, though, was thinking about Sibyl using the distraction of this meeting to slip upstairs to the archives for the night. That downright terrified him— and yeah, he communicated terror through an expression of annoyance.

"What swords?" he growled when Dillon chose weapons. "You can't even lift mine."

"Yours?" Charles reacted just as Smith had predicted—insulted, yes, but with a smarmy condescen-

sion. "The sword of Charlemagne is a relic. Even were I to choose one-handed broadswords, we wouldn't use that."

He considered it in that snotty way of his, then said, "Sabers. I'll provide them."

Score! No foils, which Trace hated. The can't-even-lift insult had struck home.

Sometimes, Smith was so conniving that he made Trace uncomfortable. But he'd planned out this exchange perfectly. Now Smith drooped his shoulders even lower, as if he could die of shame. It was an act. A good one.

Trace thought about Sibyl and about the fact that after tonight, she would have no use for him again. He glowered.

For Sibyl, the hardest part of infiltrating the Comitatus archives wasn't the security. Not once she learned where the papers were kept—a hidden room high in the New Orleans Arsenal. Not when she had Dillon Charles himself turning the alarms off, then on, first to enter the building, then to allow the Texas exiles in, and finally to leave again, to prepare for the morning's duel.

No, the hardest part was when she hesitated at the top of the blocky stone steps, watching through a piece of old iron grillwork, as Trace formally challenged Dillon Charles to a duel for possession of that old sword.

Trace might not be wielding the sword of Charlemagne for her. But he was willing to wager that sword. He was suffering through the impediments of propriety and condescension not for the sword, which he would never have risked on his own. *For her.*

To give her this time with the archives, which she'd all but demanded.

She watched him like she might a bull in a pen, allowing Smith to keep him in check, but just barely. She knew him well enough to recognize his frustration with the ritual.

Knew him…? When had that happened?

Wasn't their problem that she hadn't known him? Couldn't know someone of Comitatus blood?

No, she reminded herself, sprinting the rest of the way up the stone stairs. She had to be ready to breach this next door when Charles disabled the alarm to leave. No.

The problem was the same it had always been.

The problem was bigger than just Trace's father, despite him being the man who'd sentenced her—as a child!—to years behind bars. If this were just a matter of Trace's father…well, Trace hated his father. He might choose her if only to flaunt his independence from the Judge.

But the whole society of men, some perhaps as decent as the exiles, but more of them corrupt? The whole history of them? Bloodlines running back to ancient times, as ancient as patriarchy. As hierarchy. As conquest?

She had to let all of them know what they'd done was not acceptable. She had to destroy them completely. And when you destroyed something, you didn't keep some of it for yourself, just because you might have feelings for it. What if they did finally make love? What if she ever were impregnated by him…by the very blood she hated?

No. She'd promised her murdered father's memory that she would avenge him. Men weren't the only people with honor.

Her word meant something, too.

So she picked the physical lock on the thick wooden door to the upstairs archives. She waited for the deep voices downstairs to finally move toward the exit, then for the faint beep that—according to Smith—would signal the alarm system temporarily dropping. When she heard it, she pulled open the door, using both hands and all her strength, and slipped into the second-floor room.

She shut the door behind her. When the alarm system beeped again, she knew she was stuck here until morning—and that she'd shut all hope of rescue out. Not that she needed doors to shut people out.

Besides, she hadn't started this quest with backup. No reason she should end it that way. And even by the faint glow of French Quarter lights through slits in the blocky Arsenal wall—slits just large enough to fire arrows or flintlock muskets at the ground below—she could see that she'd all but reached the end of her quest.

She'd struggled for so long to piece together the most basic facts about the Comitatus. She'd compared genealogies and microfilmed newspaper articles. She'd hacked deeper and deeper into personal accounts and financials. She'd looked at what schools what trust fund boys had attended, and who counted as legacy enrollments. She'd made assumptions, then struggled to support those assumptions, struggled for every tidbit of confirmable intelligence. She'd met in secret, at great risk, with people who knew of the Comitatus, as well as many more who knew even less than she did.

For years. And now...

Glass-fronted bookshelves surrounded her. Wooden filing cabinets rose to the ceiling. Even apothecary cabinets, with small drawers the right size to hold scrolls, surrounded her. She could smell the familiar, dusty scent of old documents, original documents, primary sources. A conspiracy theorist's dream.

If she couldn't find the proof of her father's murder—certainly of the reasons for the cover-up—here, she would never find it.

So why was she suddenly so terrified to begin?

Trace loved the city of New Orleans. He'd loved it well before the disaster of Katrina—the evacuations, the overcrowding of refugees, the floods, the neglect. He loved the strength with which the people who remained worked to rebuild it.

The French Quarter, which housed the Arsenal, was the oldest part of the city and sat on the highest land. It had escaped the worst damage. It shone as a bright, jazzy reminder of all the city had been, was, and would be again.

And Trace didn't care about going back to it.

Smith and Mitch did, along with Arden and Val,

who'd flown in from Dallas to support Sibyl. The four of them had tried to talk Trace into accompanying them on a night out in the Quarter, at least for a drink—especially Val, who didn't want their outing to seem like a double date. They knew he would be worried.

He couldn't do it. Not with the knowledge of Sibyl, all alone, locked away in a secret chamber all night.

He no longer trusted Comitatus guards not to kill her if they found her.

Maybe he'd never trusted them to do the right thing.

So his friends headed for Bourbon Street—to, as Mitch put it, "eat, drink and be merry, for tomorrow we duel."

But Trace kept his own kind of vigil across the street from the Arsenal. As if he might sense if she needed him.

Not that she would. Sibyl had made that clear.

Trace was the last person Sibyl needed in her life.

Upstairs in the archives, though, curled on the dusty wooden floor with a sheaf of papers in her hand, Sibyl wept as she hadn't wept since she was twelve years old.

She wished she had someone to hold her. And she knew it was her quest for this exact piece of information that had robbed her of any such possibility.

The Comitatus had never held a grudge against her or her father. The Daine family had been less than enemies. They were mere pawns. Nobodies. Nothings. And by devoting her life to vengeance against the Comitatus, keeping nothing for herself or her future, she'd allowed them to make her just that.

Nobody.

She'd given vengeance her life…and now she had nothing.

Chapter 12

"Handled internally."

Two lives—her father's fiery murder and the loss of her own youth, family and future—had been reduced to two cold, final words.

"Handled internally."

Eventually, Sibyl pushed herself off the polished archive floor. She wiped her damp cheeks with fingers made gritty from all the papers she'd examined, knowing she probably left muddy stains on her face, hardly caring. She felt exhausted. Not stayed-up-half-the-night-researching exhausted, but wasted-her-life-for-information-that-didn't-bring-Daddy-back exhausted. Because she'd been right about one thing. No, the Comitatus had held no particular grudge against the Daine family line.

She read it in Dillon Charles' own words, an affidavit

of sorts. Not the Dillon Charles she knew now—adult lawyer, acquirer of swords. But the Dillon he'd once been, one who'd seemed so old and confident to the twelve-year-old scholarship student she'd once been.

One who, as she read his words, came across as seventeen years old and just plain scared.

As well he should have been.

He and others at the Academy had resented Sibyl's presence at their prep school…a school that had only started admitting girls several years earlier. A school that had been almost exclusively reserved for the privileged among the New Orleans elite. Oh, sure, granting scholarships gave them tax benefits and good publicity. But those scholarship students weren't supposed to be in the running for valedictorian. And they certainly shouldn't have been in a position to turn in their more privileged classmates for cheating.

Cheating…?

Sitting on the floor, surrounded by looming shelves and cabinets, Sibyl remembered how honored she'd felt when someone as rich and charming as Dillon Charles had suggested they all study together. She'd had so few friends, and she'd just started noticing boys. She remembered…she remembered asking where they got the practice tests.

She'd actually wondered that—where had they gotten such thorough examples? It hadn't occurred to her, even as she'd completed the answers for them, that these might not have been practice tests at all. Not even when she asked their instructor about it, after the test, only to have Dillon sweep her away from the older man's look of confusion.

She'd begun to figure it out, then. She'd begun to suspect that he'd gotten her to help cheat. But she hadn't wanted to believe it—and then the fire that night, and the news of her father's death, and the accusations...

She'd forgotten the rest—the cheating—had even happened.

Dillon hadn't.

"We figured if we spray painted some stuff about rich guys and being stuck up, and if the fire started in her locker, then she'd get kicked out for vandalism," he'd written in the affidavit. "We didn't realize there'd be an explosion. It was an accident. Nobody was meant to get hurt. It's just—they didn't belong there. And now I've messed up everything."

After which followed commentary in other hands, signed with initials instead of full names, agreeing that boys with such important futures ahead of them didn't deserve to have their lives ruined for teenaged foolishness.

For an accident.

"Handled internally," it ended.

Which she knew meant: we framed someone else. Someone unimportant. For a crime that didn't matter.

Because the Daines *didn't* have important futures ahead of them.

Or so the Comitatus had thought.

Now Sibyl stuffed the crumpled pages into her courier bag. Assuming the Comitatus didn't own every newspaper or news outlet—and they certainly didn't own the internet!—she would make sure that this cover-up was thoroughly uncovered.

But it wasn't enough. Not even close.

Rage filled her, like bile. Hatred. Injustice. It needed to explode, just like the incendiary device they'd planted in her locker. It needed to destroy their world the way they'd destroyed hers.

She had to find more evidence against them. Worse evidence. Enough for a *60 Minutes* exposé. Enough for *Dateline* and *Nightline* and Senate Intelligence investigations and independent counsels. She began throwing open file drawers at random, rifling through document after document, casting the ones she didn't want on the floor. She needed a smoking gun—smokier and even more incriminating than her own setup, since people could claim too much bias in her exposing that one.

The Comitatus had become a mildewed, decaying structure full of spiders and snakes and roaches and rats, and it was time someone shone light on their activities. Sunlight was the best disinfectant, after all.

She hesitated and looked around at the mess she'd created, papers strewn atop papers, documents as old as a hundred, two hundred, three hundred years.

Original documents.

Irreplaceable documents.

And it occurred to her. Sunlight, as a disinfectant, worked slowly.

Fire, on the other hand…

The thought frightened even her. She drew a fist to

her mouth, let the sheaf she clutched drift to the littered floor like a handful of dead leaves.

Fire would destroy it all, beyond any hope of replacement—everything except the most incriminating documents, which she would spirit away. The secrecy of the Comitatus likely led to their reluctance to keep photocopies or digital backups.

Why not use that against them?

She'd served six years in juvenile detention for a fire she'd never set. This might not count as double jeopardy—different fire, different times and she was an adult. But she knew how to leave no proof.

Sibyl's survival instincts, the same instincts that had kept her alive behind bars and paranoid even after her release, protested—but she protested back. She had the ammunition to keep those noble villains from trying to hurt her or hers, ever again.

All she had to do was wait until dawn. Light the fire in person—more sensibly than Dillon Charles had ever tried to light his—and then slip downstairs. When Dillon, arriving for his duel, disengaged the alarm system, she would slip out.

That should buy the fire time before anybody recognized what was happening. Enough time to do serious damage upstairs while, because of the tendency of heat to rise, the men downstairs should stay relatively safe.

Immediately she thought of Trace—and of Smith, and of Mitch. They'd be here, of course. *For her.* She couldn't put them in danger.

So warn them. She could telephone them as soon as she was safely away, before the fire could become a true hazard. She'd let them know what was going on, ask them to cancel the duel and get out. That would buy her archive-hungry flame even more time to do maximum damage before it was discovered.

Part of her feared what she would become, if she did this.

The larger part of her knew she'd already become worse—because of the Comitatus. This would be no less than justice.

Handled internally?

She just had to find a way to distract herself over the next few hours before dawn. Sabotage the fire alarms, of course. And collect the most incriminating examples—the examples that would most blatantly out the Comitatus secrecy to the world—before torching the rest.

Which meant reading.

Which was fine.

Sibyl never minded a night reading....

"You'd fight better if you'd gotten some sleep," noted Smith, emerging from the early morning mist to where Trace still stood, watching the blocky, looming Arsenal.

The French Quarter was never more peaceful than this, the early morning. The parties had wound down. The bars had closed. The hookers were sleeping off their night's work. In the early morning, the age of this place crept back.

Buildings two and three hundred years old. Cobblestone walks. Private courtyards. Wrought iron balconies and French doors with the original, imperfect glass.

And what was basically a fortress.

"I don't need sleep to fight." Trace rolled his shoulders as he pushed away from the wall. "Is it time?"

"Not quite." Smith surprised him by handing him a cardboard cup of coffee. Like Trace really wasn't beneath him. Like they were just friends. "I wanted to check on you first."

They sipped their hot, Louisiana coffee in tense, mist-draped silence.

Trace looked around them. "You think maybe I had noble ancestors walking around here once?"

"You're Judge LaSalle's kid, aren't you? No matter what name you take, you've got his bloodline. Sure you did."

Trace tried to imagine it. Important men, wealthy men, only a few generations beyond the time of knights in armor, striding around the city that had been cleared out of the swamp. Men with critical decisions to make. Men responsible not just for themselves, but for their communities, the way the Comitatus should have been.

The way Smith insisted they could someday be again.

"You think they were worth anything?" He looked back at his friend. "Not, you know, in dollars or francs or whatever…."

Smith considered him. "I know we tease you a lot, Trace. You—" He grinned. "You kind of make it easy."

Trace scowled.

Smith feinted a step back, as if to dodge a blow, but he was still grinning. He wasn't afraid. "But you're still one of the more impressive guys I've ever met. You knew what you were giving up, when we quit the society. Mitch and I could only imagine, but you knew, because you'd escaped it once already. And you did it." He snapped his fingers. "Like that."

Okay, now this was getting mushy. Trace shrugged and looked back up at the Arsenal. He hoped Sibyl had found what she needed.

"Judge LaSalle may be a lost cause," Smith said. "But you sure as hell don't take after him. So yeah. Somewhere back there in your family line, there have to be some heroes. Here."

Trace hesitated to look back, unsure what to do with the blatant praise. But Smith nudged him—sort of—so he looked.

Smith was holding out the aluminum case that held the sword. Maybe it was the sword of Charlemagne, maybe not. But it was his now.

Mine.

"You sure you want to risk it?" his friend asked as a cheerful hello announced Mitch's arrival. "As long as Dillon disarms the security system, so Sibyl can get out, we don't have to go through with the duel."

Trace looked at the quiet, misty streets around him... and he could almost sense the presence of some kind of great-great-grandfather who might have still cared about duty and honor and all that other stuff.

"Nah," he said, taking the sword. Even through the

case, its weight felt right in his hand. "I said I'd fight. I'll fight.

"Besides." And he grinned at his friends as wolfishly as he could. "I'm kind of curious about who'll win."

It's time, whispered Sibyl's need for vengeance. She'd fed it, counted on it for so long—for years—that it almost had its own personality. *Finally time.*

She kept skimming the scrolls on her lap, cross-referencing them to the ones she'd sorted beside her, reaching up for more. Just a while longer…

Start the fire now, or you won't get out while they're coming in.

"Don't hurry me," she whispered, and only then truly noticed her internal debate. Maybe she finally had cracked. But more likely, she just needed more time.

A society that had taken millennia to develop couldn't be dismissed in mere seconds.

Or mere hours.

Besides, she'd found something.

Actually, she'd found *lots* of somethings. Her courier bag was stuffed with incriminating documents from the nineties, the eighties, the seventies. She'd found a few tasty scandals from the sixties, the fifties, the forties.

But then, as she'd worked chronologically backward, something interesting began to happen.

The scandals and incriminations became fewer and farther between.

The voices caught within male penmanship from generations ago showed more and more…honor.

Concern.

Conflict.

And, the further she went back in time: Heroes. She found references to El Cid of Spain and Roland of France, to Lord Guan of China and Prince Yamato Takeru of Japan, to Beowulf and Charlemagne and Siegfried and the Arthurian knights. More recently—as in, post-Renaissance—she found references to explorers, founding fathers, governors, generals.

"Smith was right," she whispered. "Smith, and Mitch, and Greta…they were right."

The Comitatus had once been something wonderful.

Once, insisted her need for vengeance. *No more.* Which was true. Nobody knew how true more intensely than did she. And yet, seeing what they'd once been, she could page forward through time with more insight.

Those men of noble blood, men who'd descended from heroes, had honestly strived for generations to live up to their past. They had founded and funded charities. They had spoken up against injustices from the horror of slavery to the threat, and occasional necessity, of war.

They hadn't always been evil.

And as members within their ranks had slowly turned further and further from philanthropy and heroics, and more and more toward elitism and pragmatism, it hadn't been a simple change. Even men named Charles and LaSalle had protested that they might need to risk their existence to protect the core of decency among them. But as times had changed, as new generations replaced the old, fewer and fewer of those protests had found voice.

More than once, Sibyl had come across documents with a surprising "kids these days" tone, be they from the 1920s or the 1840s. More than once, she found documents in which men debated the common sense of maintaining pure honor, if that honor might lead to the society's destruction. Many felt that without honor, they didn't deserve to continue.

More—and more often—chose pragmatism.

They weren't one body. They weren't one mind. Not everybody in the Comitatus had betrayed her—the New Orleans powers had. In Dallas, Arden Leigh's father had lost his life pursuing belated honor. Smith Donnell's father, even now, seemed to be doing what he could to help his son without breaking his own vows. And then there were Smith, and Mitch….

And Trace. Exiles, yes. But exiled for a reason.

The Comitatus weren't an army—they were an organization. Powerful, yes, and everyone knew what absolute power could do. And yet, if they could somehow be salvaged…?

Ridiculous. Stupid. She needed vengeance, didn't she?

But did that vengeance need to come at the cost of the exiles' idealism? Did it really need to come at the cost of Trace's belief in himself? Or did the cycle of violence have to end somewhere? And who, really, did she want to risk?

Dillon Charles hadn't thought anybody would be hurt, in the fire he set. And Sibyl had it in her power to be not just nothing, but nothing like Dillon Charles.

Pink light slanted through the south-facing balistrariae, across the chaos her search had created. Dawn. She wouldn't hear voices in the street until the door opened; the walls of the Arsenal were too thick. Once the door opened, that was her chance to slip out of the archives without setting off any bells.

So what, exactly, would she take with her?

And what did she plan on leaving behind?

Chapter 13

"We will use the Renaissance *code duello,*" announced Dillon Charles, and gave Trace an over-exaggerated look of sympathy. "That means the dueling code."

"Ya think?" Trace wondered how badly it would break the *code duello* to just KO the jerk and be done with it. But Mitch and Smith had given him a refresher course on the rules, just in case. Apparently, an honorable second was not above killing his own man if that man cheated.

True, his friends' honor had already been compromised. But why risk it?

"Yes," agreed Dillon, pacing across the glossy, dark wood floor. "I see you brought both your seconds. As you can see, I have mine. And David, over there, is a doctor."

David held up a hand briefly.

"As agreed yestereve—" yeah, he actually said *yestereve* "—we're too civilized to go for either first blood or duels to the death, tempting or not. So we're fighting to ten touches, yes?"

Smith agreed while Trace glanced toward the stone stairway, wishing he knew if Sibyl had found what she needed. Whether she had or not, she needed him to use this duel to stall, so that she could sneak back out to safety. So as much as he wanted to just get to the slashing-stabbing-violence part of the morning, he merely shifted his weight and let Dillon blather on.

This was him stalling.

"Most duels are to start with a final attempt at reconciliation," continued Dillon, as if this was some college class instead of a freakin' fight. "You challenged me, though I'm the injured party."

Trace let his scowl refute that part.

"You took something, which doesn't belong to you." Dillon looked coolly at the sword case. "Speaking of which…?"

Mitch opened the aluminum case to reveal, on egg carton-shell foam lining, the ancient blade. No way were either of them fighting without the proof that their prize, the sword, waited for the victor.

"Unless my dad was screwing around with your mom and we're half brothers," noted Trace, "it belongs to me."

He enjoyed Dillon's obvious distaste at the idea.

"No reconciliation, then." Dillon set his mouth in that most annoying way of his. "Good. We've taken the liberty of pacing off the piste—that would be the fighting area, Beaudry—although we marked the corners with painter's tape instead of handkerchiefs. More practical, don't you think? Anybody who steps out of bounds is deemed a coward and, of course, receives a penalty."

Trace folded his arms. "Can I hurt you now?"

"Stop it," snapped Smith—who'd luckily warned Trace that he'd be playing the sympathetic-to-Dillon role for their morning's entertainment. *Good cop,* without the legal overtones. "These rituals may not matter to *you*—"

"It's quite all right," Dillon assured him. "I knew what to expect from this one already. Luckily, size and bluster tends to be a weakness in fencing, not a strength. Morgan?"

One of his seconds—a silver spoon type who somehow fit his girly name—knelt and opened three long, wooden boxes. In each lay a pair of fencing sabers.

"As we brought the weapons, you may choose which you prefer."

Nice of him. While Trace preferred the weight of a saber over the wimpier épée or foil, sabers boasted curved hand guards that sometimes cramped his large hands. He tried one, then another and nodded when he found one that he could grip comfortably.

It would be easier to accept Dillon's brand of honor, though, if Trace believed it would apply to him without Smith and Mitch here. Or if Dillon had shown any—at all—to the innocent Sibyl had been!

"You know the rules of sabers, of course," Dillon

said, as Morgan cleared the boxes from the floor. "You can hit with any part of the sword, but only attacks above the waist score points. There's still time to fetch electronic scoring equipment, if you don't want to trust our seconds to—"

"Can we fight now?" interrupted Trace. This was why he liked no-holds-barred fights. The recitation of rules after standards after rituals could drive a man bat-crap crazy. He'd fenced in college. He would remember, more or less.

Dillon drew himself up to his full height, lip curling. "Fine, then."

And he turned, walked back to the center stripe of tape and turned, assuming the appropriate pose with his sword in the air and his left hand on his hip. "En garde."

Trace lifted his own sword and nodded, his silent salute a rebellion against the fancy rules. He also didn't put his hand on his hip, because that just looked stupid. He kept it behind him.

Dillon advanced in quick, short steps.

Trace crossed the floor with longer strides, pointing his saber ahead of him to signal his attack, giving him right of way, and swung toward his opponent's side. When Dillon raised his sword—Trace could imagine him reciting, *position one*—Trace veered his own strike and thwacked the villain in the neck with the side of the blade. "Point."

"Ow!" Dillon let go of his hip then, to rub his neck. "You don't get points for how hard you hit!"

"Nah." Trace grinned his anger. "It's just more fun that way. On guard yourself."

And the fight really started.

For her.

To the rhythmic, cymbal sound of blade on blade, Sibyl leaned around the corner, outside the archive door, and watched. Dillon Charles might be fighting for the sword Trace had found. But not Trace.

Trace had only offered up the sword, called for the duel, *for her.*

Glad that she hadn't set a fire, that she wouldn't have to hurry, she sank in the shadow against the stone wall and tried to grasp the import of this. Both men moved all over the piste, Dillon in a kind of dance, Trace in a predatory stalk, with their seconds dodging back and forth at the edges to keep track of the thrusts and parries. The choreography of it dated back centuries, millennia.

And this time it was over her?

After Trace's aggression first caught Dillon by surprise, Dillon quickly recovered. The fight was more evenly matched now. Dillon was clearly the more elegant fencer, protecting an almost perfect three-inch radius between his parrying sword and his body, advancing and retreating along so clear a line that it might as well have been drawn on the floor for him. He varied his short and long steps, sometimes even executing a full ballestra—a two-footed hop into a showy lunge.

His speed and ease with the saber served him well.

More than once, he slipped a strike past Trace's parry through simple practice.

Trace, on the other hand, lost almost as many points in penalties as he scored in hits—but his sheer belligerence held its own power. He knew to use the *forte,* or strong, lower part, of his blade to parry and attack, again and again, wearing Dillon down as the wealthier man fought him off.

My champion, Sibyl thought, more impressed by Trace's raw strength than she ever would be by elegance. She knew better than to trust elegance, but Trace's fighting held…honesty. *He's not always right. But he's always trying.*

"What's the matter?" demanded Trace, after scoring a point with a sharp whip against Dillon's side, then losing it by "missing" and hitting his leg. "Was that too hard? I can be more gentle."

"Funny," spat Dillon. "That's what I told your girl-friend, but she said she likes it rough."

Sibyl straightened, surprised. She wished she were psychic, so she could let Trace know the truth. *He's making it up. He's making it up. He doesn't even know for sure that we—*

With a snarl, Trace bodychecked Dillon right out of the piste and onto his butt.

"Unsportsmanlike conduct!" protested one of Dillon's seconds. "Corp-a-corps!"

Rather than defending Trace's points, though, Mitch and Smith were dragging their friend back before he could fall on the downed Comitatus like a grizzly onto a beached salmon. That Trace didn't swipe them away with one paw said he had more control than Sibyl had feared.

But he still played into Dillon's taunt when he warned, "Don't talk about her that way. Not after what you did to her."

That's all Dillon needed. "Me? What kind of lies has Isabel been telling you?" He allowed his own friends to help him up, brushed off his fencing whites. "She's the one who served time in prison, Beaudry. She's the firebug. Ask the Judge."

"You told me what you did to her!"

"Did I? As if your word holds any validity among real gentlemen?" Again, Dillon raised his sword. "*En guarde,* bastard."

"Oh, I'm on guard, you hoity wimp." Again, Trace attacked aggressively, just shy of losing more points… in part, Sibyl thought, because of Dillon's reluctance to complain.

Your funeral.

Still, Dillon's tongue cut as sharply as any blade. "The trailer trash and the ex-con. You two should have your own reality show, because that's all you're any good for. Entertainment."

Clash. Slash. Turn. Trace growled, but said nothing. *Not good with words,* he'd told Sibyl once. Watching, her own throat tight, she wondered how sharply he felt that. How much was he suffering for her?

"Leave the things of real importance—" Dillon parried one of Trace's attacks, struggling to push away the weight of it without using his illegal left hand for ballast "—like the sword of Charlemagne, to the heroes who deserve it."

And that, she couldn't let pass.

Sibyl stepped away from the wall, into full view of the men below. "The sword of Roland!"

Dillon's expression of shock, as he looked up at her, was priceless.

Even better when Trace, who'd known she would be near, whapped him upside the head with his saber. "Point. I win."

"That's…you can't…!" Now Dillon's attention pivoted between Sibyl, as she descended the stone steps, and Trace, as he stepped forward to claim the weapon that had begun all this. The seconds, and the doctor, didn't help the confusion by launching into a cacophony of complaints— on the Comitatus side—and defenses, on the exiles'.

Sibyl watched how Trace hefted the antique blade, far better fit to his size and power than the slim saber had been. At that moment, he didn't just look like a knight. He looked like her knight.

Some of them could be champions and heroes, after all.

He lifted his gaze to hers. "The sword of who?"

"Roland," she repeated, reaching the gleaming wood floor and making a beeline for him. He closed the space to her, caught her to him. For a moment, she dared to hope there might still be a chance for them—but no. He drew her behind him for her own safety, so she talked between his ribs and his arm. "I told you about him before, after I did my research, didn't I? Hero of the *Song of Roland*. His sacrifice saved France—and Charlemagne—from the Saracens. Dillon should know that."

She peeked around the sturdy, warm wall that was Trace and made a face at the man who'd tried to ruin her life…but, she now thought, had only put it in stasis. Like an evil spell, until her prince woke her.

"It was in the archives," she added.

Smith had grabbed the dueling saber Trace had dropped, protectively flanking them on one side. "Uh, Sibyl? You were supposed to sneak out, not make a speech."

Mitch backed to the other side, with little more for defense than one of the wooden boxes. "You ever hear that saying about how they'd tell you but then they'd have to kill you? You ever wonder where that came from?"

"Your family may be loosely connected to Charlemagne," Sibyl continued to Dillon, having found her voice at long last. "But Trace's bloodline goes directly back to Roland. Generations back, records show the LaSalles owning the sword of Roland. It's Trace's sword, and you've known it all along."

"That just makes it the Judge's sword," insisted Dillon.

"Which gives you more of a claim *how?*"

"Don't you dare accuse me of dishonor, you bitch!"

Trace surged forward. Smith, Mitch and Sibyl barely held him back.

"You want to talk dishonor?" Dillon accused. "All of you broke your vows! And to tell our secrets to an outsider, a *woman!* That could be a blood offense, even if you were in good standing!"

"Told you so," Mitch grunted, still struggling to hold Trace back.

Rather than pulling from behind, Sibyl slipped in front of Trace—and sure enough, he stopped his struggle rather than risk pushing her into Dillon. While Trace tried to sweep her back again, too gently to succeed, she took a moment to truly look at the man—the boy—who had ruined her life.

What a...nobody.

"Hold them!" insisted Dillon to his friends. "Call the police—I know Captain Harrison. We need to convene an emergency meeting and demand—"

But he stopped when Sibyl closed the distance between them in a quick run, and jumped. She caught one boot against Dillon's chest, giving her the footing she needed to kick the other, hard, off his face before springing back to land on her feet.

Dillon sprawled onto his back, like a felled tree.

When Dillon's seconds tried to rush her, Smith elbowed one in the gut and Mitch clotheslined the other. Trace, in the meantime, *lifted* Sibyl away so that he loomed between her and the half conscious Dillon, one big arm protecting her shoulder and side like armor.

In his other hand, he still held his ancestral sword.

"These men didn't tell me anything," Sibyl told everyone, speaking loudly to be heard over the continuing scuffles. "Not Smith, not Mitch, not Trace. You know who gave away the existence of the Comitatus? *Him!*"

And she pointed downward.

"Nuh…!" protested Dillon, spitting out some blood with the word as he tried to pull himself onto his elbows. His doctor sank to his knees beside him, trying to check his pulse, examining his injuries.

"Uh-huh!" Sibyl insisted. "Back when you had your father frame me for the fire *you* started, the death *you* caused. It was all too pat. Too many important people believed the lie on less than circumstantial evidence. Too many parole hearings went against me. The Comitatus tied it up so neatly, *I* almost believed it!"

But Trace hadn't. He hadn't believed.

She leaned into the brace of his side, under the shelter of his arm. Right where, despite her earlier fears, she hoped she might stay.

"So I started researching," she continued. "Trying to understand. And I found the Comitatus. I found them before I ever found the exiles. And I would've destroyed you, too—if it weren't for the hope that these guys have given me."

She looked way, way up. One guy in particular.

Trace tipped his face, swarthy and whisker-shadowed, toward hers. Then he used his free hand to pivot her, scoop her up and against him, and finally covered her mouth with his. And…yes.

Sibyl had thought the kisses in his bedroom had moved her world. But now that she knew everything, now that she trusted Trace for who he was—a warrior, a hero, a *man*—and not despite it, she all but dissolved against him. Why not let him take over? Why not sink into his strength, open herself to his power, be his?

If, after all her mistakes, he was willing to be hers.

Her arms wrapped around the back of his neck, to hold herself up. Her legs wrapped around his waist, her calves hard against his tight, blue-jeaned butt. His tongue invaded, conquered, and she welcomed him.

Yes…

Until a sudden lurch, accompanied by Trace's sudden abandonment of her mouth, woke her back to the moment. And to the fact that Trace had seen something suspicious from Dillon, even in the midst of that incredible kiss. Trace now had the sword of Roland against Dillon's throat.

Dillon dropped the saber he'd managed to pick up, during their distraction.

For perhaps the first time since childhood, here in the lair of the Comitatus, Sibyl felt safe.

"What do you want, Sib?" Trace asked, his voice rough and merciless—toward Dillon. The free arm that still held her to his broad chest almost cuddled her, in contrast. "Tell me what you want me to do."

Slowly, Sibyl unlocked her ankles and slid back down his body until her boots hit the gleaming floor. She kind of wanted to kick the jerk again. But considering the situation they were in, she had a better idea.

"Make him confess publicly. Please. I know what happened, logically. I've read his version of it in the archives. But I…I want to hear him say it. I want *them* to hear it."

The bulging muscles in Trace's arm barely flexed, but Dillon whimpered.

"You heard the lady." Trace smiled. "Talk."

From somewhere behind them, Mitch said, "Let me get my camera phone…got it!"

And Dillon talked.

Sibyl didn't realize just how badly she'd needed this, nor for how long, until she felt the tears dripping off her chin—and felt Trace wipe them away with one rough thumb.

Chapter 14

He probably shouldn't have kissed her.

With the impression of her lips still tingling on his, Trace had a hard time fully appreciating that. But he had a hard time appreciating algebra and physics, too. That didn't make them any less true.

She'd already said she didn't want any more to do with him, after learning he'd kept Dillon's secret. She'd been vulnerable just now. So he shouldn't have kissed her, no matter how sexy he found her determination here, in the midst of Comitatus territory, or her beautifully executed kick to Dillon's face.

No matter how certain the sword of Roland made him feel in his grip, between him and their enemy.

Vulnerable, he had to remind himself.

He only learned just *how* vulnerable when Dillon Charles began his halting confession. Sibyl had already told the story. Her father's death. Her imprisonment. But hearing it from Dillon's mouth…!

The idiot tried to make himself the victim?

"I was stupid," he admitted—of the cheating. "I didn't understand honor yet. I was…scared."

Yeah, like with the tip of the sword of Roland against his throat he was scared? Trace considered how easy it would be to just slip. A tiny cut to the carotid artery, and *splash*. Vengeance for Sibyl.

But Sibyl lay her small, soft hand on his sword arm, just barely shook her head. "What about the adults?"

Confusion warred with Dillon's obvious fear of the sword. "What?"

"Your father prosecuted me. Judge LaSalle convicted me. The school administrators, the police, the parole boards. They weren't young and scared, were they? Assuming fear was even a good excuse for doing what you did."

Dillon's face, strained up and away from the blade, seemed to seek the right answer. But his mouth formed nothing Trace could hear.

"They were cruel," Sibyl answered for him. "No, worse…they were *indifferent*. The ancient code of the Comitatus gave them wealth and power because they were best suited to manage it, because they needed it to take care of everyone else. Even at your most 'honorable,' did you ever put the less fortunate ahead of yourself? Not just me—twelve years old, my father dead, falsely convicted. Anyone?"

Dillon's mouth opened. Closed. Twisted with misery.

"I didn't think so."

And Sibyl turned her back on the man who'd ruined her life, and she tipped her gaze to Trace's. "That's it. Thank you. I'm done."

But he didn't lower his sword. He wouldn't trust Dillon with something as precious as Sibyl, even if this *was* it. If she *were* done…with everything Comitatus.

Including him.

"He needs to do more," Trace insisted. "He needs to promise you'll be safe."

When Dillon made a gargling noise, Smith said, "I don't think he can promise anything until he can talk again."

So Trace pulled the sword back. Just barely.

"She's the one who trespassed!" Dillon's hand, flying to his throat, left a slight, red smear. Oops. "You're the ones who helped her. And you're asking us for favors?"

Sibyl caught Trace's arm before he could silence the jerk with his sword again. "For justice. There's a difference."

"Let's call the police and press charges, and you'll see justice! With your record?" He pointed at Sibyl, then pointed at Trace. "And your…your brutality? We'll…"

But he trailed off against the sound of his own disembodied voice. "…so I got her locker's combination out of the headmaster's office, and I snuck in after hours to set it up. I got the instructions out of one of those anarchist crazy books—can of spray paint, timer, stuff like that—and I figured, hey, it'd just be a little explosion…."

Mitch silenced his cell phone's playback, and whistled. "Fifty-seven hits already on the video-sharing site where I posted it. I sure hope you don't belong to some group that could be implicated in your confession there, Dillon."

Dillon's face flushed as he leapt to his feet, practically ignoring the sword now. "You *common narc!*"

"Nah, that would be Trace. The common part, not the narc part. No offense."

"None taken," grunted Trace to his friend—and kept the sword of Roland cleanly between Dillon and the others.

"I," Mitch reminded everyone, "am one of the blue bloods. Oh, well. Guess we aren't as perfect as we like to think. Sixty-two hits."

"I've got connections!" Dillon insisted, his movements increasingly wide, increasingly less controlled. "I know people in the District Attorney's office!"

"Not as well as you think." That was Dillon's friend Morgan, the one with the pretty face. "And some of us with the D.A. sure as hell don't know you. Look—" This he said, turning to Sibyl and the exiles. "I can't promise to control everyone. You should probably stay out of the state for a while, just to be safe. But this young woman has suffered far more than anyone should have to, just to cover someone else's butt. As long as I'm in the Comitatus, I'll fight any motions for retribution. Agreed?"

Sibyl said nothing. And Trace was pretty sure Morgan was talking to her.

"Ms. Daine?" he prompted.

Just as Trace began to really worry, Sibyl asked, "How do I know I can trust you?"

Morgan winced. Dillon's other second said, "Because we take honor seriously." Dr. David rolled his eyes at the foolishness of that statement.

Morgan said, "I don't know how to convince you that people like Dillon Charles, here—and the folks who helped him—are the exception instead of the rule. That some of us really are striving for decency. I don't know who to hold up as an example...."

Which is when Sibyl looked over her shoulder at Smith, at Mitch—and, longest, at Trace. "I'd do anything for at least one of you."

Did she mean...

Then she turned back to Morgan and offered her hand. "I agree."

Things got blurry for Sibyl after that. Not while it was happening—the adrenaline of her situation, of the breaking and entering, of the stolen papers in her bag, of the swordfight, gave the next few hours a clarity so sharp, it might have been in high definition.

Morgan—and Smith—left together with Dillon, to allow him the small dignity of turning himself in rather than face a public arrest. According to Morgan, the statute of limitations for Dillon's arson would have run out, had nobody died in the fire. Because of the manslaughter of Sibyl's father, Dillon Charles would most certainly face charges.

It wasn't enough. It wouldn't bring her daddy back, or mend her broken family, or return her lost years.

But it was more than Sibyl had ever truly believed she would get.

Mitch made a quick phone call to Arden Leigh and Val Diaz, who met them for coffee and beignets in a café along the Mississippi River. To Sibyl's surprise, Arden gave her a big, earnest hug and a kiss on the cheek, and even Val clapped her on the shoulder and said, "Way to go, kid."

As if they'd come here not to support the men, but… her?

Sibyl hadn't realized how hungry she'd gotten since sneaking into the Arsenal the evening before, until she took that first bite. While the others discussed the wisdom of heading back to Texas as soon as possible, and Mitch looked over some of the papers she'd "liberated" from the archives, Sibyl ate almost as much as Trace.

"This is amazing," Mitch exclaimed—more than once—as he examined some of the oldest documents. "Do you realize that with this, we know what families had at least ten, no, a dozen of the swords? We can go out searching for them!"

"Why?" asked Val simply. Despite her protests that she didn't care for Mitch—who obviously liked her— Sibyl noticed that Val had sat immediately across from the blond man instead of in the empty chair to the other side of Trace.

Good. *Stay away from Trace.*

"Because these swords represent what the Comi— what the Schmomitatus once was. What they can be again. Maybe if we find them, we can find other aspects of honor that we lost. Maybe even other exiles."

Which is when, just like that, the adrenaline wore off…and Sibyl felt herself sag, caffeine or no caffeine, against Trace's side.

"Yeah, well, before that, I think a couple of you need some sleep," noted Val drily.

Which was the last piece of clarity Sibyl had, until she woke up in a hotel room bed…wrapped not just in a comforter, but in the heavier, dearer warmth and weight of Trace Beaudry.

An orange light came through the high window but, not having paid attention to the hotel's orientation when he brought her back here, Sibyl had no idea if she were looking at sunrise, or sunset. How long had she slept?

And what had she done to deserve someone like Trace, protecting her even in his sleep, even after everything she'd called him, every way she'd deceived him?

The room around them could belong to any number of decent motel chains. She didn't care. It could be a honeymoon suite for all that it mattered…or a cave.

Luckily, she or someone else had taken off her cowboy boots before exhaustion had claimed her. She braced a bare foot on Trace's thick, blue-jeaned leg to give herself the leverage she needed to arch upward for his mouth and kiss his surprisingly soft, sleeping lips.

The chatter of her thoughts melted to silent bliss. Halfway through, Trace seemed to wake up. But that just resulted in a deepening of the kiss. More pressure. Tongue. He rolled while he kissed her back, all but trapping her between the mattress and the hard weight of him, but she didn't fear him. She felt safe against his masculinity, not fearful.

She also felt powerfully aroused.

"I love you," she whispered up to him, when his lips released hers long enough for them to catch their breath. His sleepy eyes, gazing down into hers, widened, but she couldn't chicken out now. "I'm sorry I wasn't honest at first. I'm sorry I was so suspicious. I lov—"

But the kiss with which he silenced her returned the sentiment tenfold. And when she tugged at his T-shirt, wanting to span her hands across his wide, hairy chest… When he slid his hands up her bare back, tugging off her shirt and rasping his cheek across her sensitive, soft breasts… When she fumbled at the waistband of his straining jeans, her thighs itchy with a need only he could soothe…

After preparing her with several juicy orgasms, Trace eventually, tenderly slid himself into her, claiming her completely for himself. When his gasps deepened into growls, his strokes turned into thrusts and his control became a shuddering shout of surrender…

Finally, Isabel "Sibyl" Daine was home.

Trace had saved her, all right.

He'd saved her from far more than she'd ever known to fear.

"I'll get rid of the sword," he whispered afterward, his voice sandpaper, as he cuddled her tenderly against his chest. "I'll stop helping Smith and Mitch. You shouldn't have to be reminded of that damned—of those damned you-know-who's…."

Even now, he was keeping his vow of secrecy to them, wasn't he? Even after she knew as much, or more, than he did.

She liked that he kept vows so well. "I like your sword," she assured him, sliding her hand down the treasure trail of dark hair that descended his abdomen to…

He gasped back a laugh. "Yeah, well that one's not going anywhere."

She snuggled closer to him, feeling delightfully risqué. "Good."

"But the other one…"

"It's the sword of Roland." She kissed him. "Not Charlemagne. I like Roland. I like his great-great-great-great…"

Considering that she kissed him after each "great," she lost count before she finished, "Grandson. He didn't need the support of Charlemagne to fight off his enemies. He had been betrayed, but he didn't let it stop him from doing what's right."

Trace spent some time kissing her back—cupping his rough hand over her breast, down the slope and over the curve of her waist, her thigh, securing her with the weight of his own heavy leg. Then he frowned at her.

"Didn't Roland die?"

"Doesn't mean he stopped doing what's right. That's why his legend goes on."

He rolled onto his back, lifting her with him so that she straddled his waist like she might a war horse. "And you think I take after him?"

But this wasn't just play, anymore. He searched her face like he really cared.

"I think," she whispered down at him, adoring every rough inch of him—and that was a lot of inches, once you added them all up—"that you're not the only one. Nothing can make up for what happened to my family, but you and your friends—even some of the Comitatus—you're making it right. I think, my love, that you're all the hero a damsel like me could ever want."

And to her delight, he proved it to her yet again.

Epilogue

"I can't get it open," muttered Sibyl in frustration, tugging at the envelope of hard plastic.

"I've got a knife." Shifting beside her on the concrete bench in Greta's now-well-tended backyard, Trace wrangled a penknife out of his pocket.

Sibyl enjoyed watching the practiced ease with which he thumbed it open. "You heroes and your blades."

"This is nothing." He made short work of the packaging around the disposable cell phone Sibyl had bought that morning. "You should see my sword."

She bit her lip, not wanting to laugh. He hadn't noticed the double entendre, which she thought was kind of cute. In fact, Trace *had* kept the sword of Roland. In the days since New Orleans, they'd begun the process of locating other Comitatus blades.

Blades that hopefully represented the good that their

society could someday regain as surely as did Smith's sword of Aeneas and Trace's sword of Roland.

But all that would happen in days to come. For now...

Sibyl stared at the disposable cell phone—for which she'd paid cash. She might feel safer with Trace than she had before, but that didn't mean she could give up all caution.

"You forget the number?" asked Trace, concern softening his brawler's face.

"It's a new number. New to me, anyway. I've never even met my stepfather. But I looked it up. I know it."

"Then what?" Apparently figuring it out, he gathered her into his lap, which Sibyl greatly appreciated. The chill from the concrete bench had begun to seep through her jeans into her butt. "You know, you don't have to do this."

"I know. I want to. I just have to stop worrying, you know? What if she doesn't want to hear from me? What if she really does blame me for dad's death? What if—"

At which point, Trace kissed her.

Sibyl sank back into the curl of his arms, the brace of his chest, kissing him back with what she hoped was practiced ease. With all the kissing they'd been doing, she *should* be good at this. But he was better. His mouth worked at hers, his tongue barely brushed the curve of her lower lip. And he loved her—he'd told her he loved her, and she hadn't doubted it, and she loved him...

And all was well. See: *happily ever after.*

As Trace finished the kiss, he pressed the new phone

back into Sibyl's hand. Half in a daze, she dialed the number and dreamily listened to it ring.

Only as a once familiar voice said hello did her thoughts flood back. She grabbed on to Trace's arm for real support.

"Hello?" asked the voice again, sounding concerned now.

Sibyl had to say something. "Mom?"

"Isabel! Oh, my—Isabel, darling! Is that really you?"

Sibyl sank into the strength of Trace, relief relaxing her throat. "It's me, Mom. Happy New Year."

* * * * *

COMING NEXT MONTH

Available January 25, 2011

#1643 NO ORDINARY HERO
Conard County: The Next Generation
Rachel Lee

#1644 IN HIS PROTECTIVE CUSTODY
The Doctors Pulaski
Marie Ferrarella

#1645 DEADLY VALENTINE
"Her Un-Valentine" by Justine Davis
"The February 14th Secret" by Cindy Dees

#1646 THE PRODIGAL BRIDE
The Bancroft Brides
Beth Cornelison

ROMANTIC SUSPENSE

REQUEST YOUR
FREE BOOKS!

2 FREE NOVELS
PLUS
2 FREE GIFTS!

ROMANTIC
SUSPENSE

Sparked by Danger, Fueled by Passion.

YES! Please send me 2 FREE Silhouette® Romantic Suspense novels and my 2 FREE gifts (gifts are worth about $10). After receiving them, if I don't wish to receive any more books, I can return the shipping statement marked "cancel." If I don't cancel, I will receive 4 brand-new novels every month and be billed just $4.24 per book in the U.S. or $4.99 per book in Canada. That's a saving of 15% off the cover price! It's quite a bargain! Shipping and handling is just 50¢ per book.* I understand that accepting the 2 free books and gifts places me under no obligation to buy anything. I can always return a shipment and cancel at any time. Even if I never buy another book from Silhouette, the two free books and gifts are mine to keep forever.

240/340 SDN E5Q4

Name	(PLEASE PRINT)	
Address		Apt. #
City	State/Prov.	Zip/Postal Code

Signature (if under 18, a parent or guardian must sign)

Mail to the **Silhouette Reader Service:**

IN U.S.A.: P.O. Box 1867, Buffalo, NY 14240-1867
IN CANADA: P.O. Box 609, Fort Erie, Ontario L2A 5X3

Not valid for current subscribers to Silhouette Romantic Suspense books.

Want to try two free books from another line?
Call 1-800-873-8635 or visit www.morefreebooks.com.

* Terms and prices subject to change without notice. Prices do not include applicable taxes. N.Y. residents add applicable sales tax. Canadian residents will be charged applicable provincial taxes and GST. Offer not valid in Quebec. This offer is limited to one order per household. All orders subject to approval. Credit or debit balances in a customer's account(s) may be offset by any other outstanding balance owed by or to the customer. Please allow 4 to 6 weeks for delivery. Offer available while quantities last.

Your Privacy: Silhouette is committed to protecting your privacy. Our Privacy Policy is available online at www.eHarlequin.com or upon request from the Reader Service. From time to time we make our lists of customers available to reputable third parties who may have a product or service of interest to you. If you would prefer we not share your name and address, please check here. ☐

Help us get it right—We strive for accurate, respectful and relevant communications. To clarify or modify your communication preferences, visit us at www.ReaderService.com/consumerchoice.

*Harlequin Romance author Donna Alward is loved
for her gorgeous rancher heroes.*

*Meet Wyatt as he's confronted by both a precious
little pink bundle left on his doorstep and his neighbor Elli
who's going to show him the ropes....*

Introducing
PROUD RANCHER, PRECIOUS BUNDLE

THE SQUAWKING QUIETED as Elli picked the baby up, and
Wyatt turned around, trying hard to ignore the feelings of
inadequacy as Darcy immediately stopped fussing.

"Maybe she's uncomfortable. What do you think, sweet-
heart?" Elli turned her conversation to the baby.

"What do you think is wrong?" Wyatt asked, putting the
coffee pot back on the burner.

A strange look passed over Elli's face, one that looked
like guilt and panic. But it was gone quickly. "I couldn't
say," she replied.

"But you were so good with her this afternoon." Wyatt
put his hands on his hips.

"Lucky, that's all. I just…remembered a few things."
The same strange look flitted over her features once more.

Wyatt took the coffee to the table. "You fooled me. You
looked like you knew exactly what you were doing." So
much so that Wyatt had felt completely inept. A feeling he
despised. He was used to being the one in control.

Elli and Darcy walked the length of the kitchen and
back. After a few moments, she admitted, "I haven't really
cared for a baby before. The things I thought of were simply
things I'd heard about. Not from experience, Mr. Black."

Her chin jutted up, closing the subject but making him

want to ask the questions now pulsing through his mind. But then he remembered the old saying—*Don't look a gift horse in the mouth.* He'd benefit from whatever insight she had and be glad of it.

"I don't really know what babies need," he said. "I fed her, patted her back like you did, walked her to sleep, but every time I put her down…"

Wyatt almost groaned. Of course. He'd forgotten one important thing. He'd been so focused on getting the formula the right temperature that he'd forgotten to check her diaper. Not that he had any clue what to do there either.

Pulling calves and shoveling out stalls was far less intimidating than one tiny newborn.

"She's probably due for a diaper change, isn't she." He tried to sound nonchalant. This was a perfect opportunity. Elli must know how to change a diaper. He could simply watch her so he'd know better for the next time.

Instead, Elli came around the corner of the counter and placed Darcy back in his arms. "Here you go, Uncle Wyatt," she said lightly. "You get diaper duty. I'll fix the coffee. Cream and sugar?"

Oh boy, Wyatt thought, looking down into Darcy's pursed face, his smug plan blown to smithereens. He was in for it now.

Will sparks fly between Elli and Wyatt?

Find out in
PROUD RANCHER, PRECIOUS BUNDLE

Available February 2011 from Harlequin Romance

Try these Healthy and Delicious Spring Rolls!

INGREDIENTS

2 packages rice-paper spring roll wrappers (20 wrappers)

1 cup grated carrot

¼ cup bean sprouts

1 cucumber, julienned

1 red bell pepper, without stem and seeds, julienned

4 green onions finely chopped— use only the green part

DIRECTIONS

1. Soak one rice-paper wrapper in a large bowl of hot water until softened.

2. Place a pinch each of carrots, sprouts, cucumber, bell pepper and green onion on the wrapper toward the bottom third of the rice paper.

3. Fold ends in and roll tightly to enclose filling.

4. Repeat with remaining wrappers. Chill before serving.

Find this and many more delectable recipes including the perfect dipping sauce in

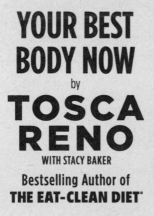

YOUR BEST BODY NOW
by
TOSCA RENO
WITH STACY BAKER
**Bestselling Author of
THE EAT-CLEAN DIET®**

Available wherever books are sold!

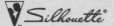

SPECIAL EDITION

FROM *USA TODAY* BESTSELLING AUTHOR

CHRISTINE RIMMER

COMES AN ALL-NEW BRAVO FAMILY TIES STORY.

Donovan McRae has experienced
the greatest loss a man can face, and
while he can't forgive himself, life—
and Abilene Bravo's love—are still
waiting for him. Can he find it in himself
to reach out and claim them?

Look for

DONOVAN'S CHILD

available February 2011